R.J. SIERRA
WEIGHT OF THE WORLD

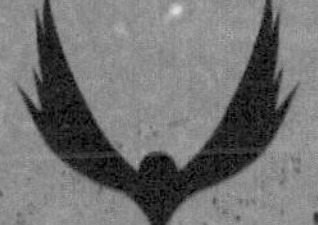

www.aethonbooks.com

ALSO IN THE SERIES

Dead to the World
World of Trouble
Weight of the World
World on Fire

You might not believe this, but I was running away. It was pouring down rain, I was soaked to the skin, and the woman chasing me through the night was cranking off shots with a semi-automatic assault rifle.

And *I*, Gaia Charmer, was running away. Which meant *Mother Earth* herself was running away.

Because, in case you didn't know, Gaia Charmer *is* Mother Earth in human form. *For real.*

Not that Crystal Ruby Hayes, the numbnuts with the rifle, knew all that. All *she* knew was that some petite blonde in her twenties with a pleated braid slung over her right shoulder had just torn up the road in front of her SUV and taken off with the bundle that Crystal had stolen days ago from a rest stop along the Pennsylvania Turnpike.

A bundle that needed its diaper changed *immediately.*

"Easy, kid," I said as the child bawled its lungs out. "I'll take care of you."

It was true. Even as Crystal fired round after round, I deflected them with a shower of rocks cast up from the ground behind me. Earth avatar that I am, I could sense every bullet's approach and fling up any part of the ground to make it ricochet harmlessly away. Not a single shell came anywhere near brushing my brown leather jacket.

But baby Mary Lou Robbins still wasn't in the clear, which was why I was running. Sprinting into the woods off the side of the road, I turned a portion of my senses forward, searching for the perfect deposit of local granite. It wasn't far, and I picked up my pace, even as Crystal kept shooting and running faster in my wake, gaining on me.

I reached out with my mind, drawing on the vast well of power within me. The granite responded, wrenching itself from under the surface to hang in the air ahead of us.

The baby shrieked in my arms as I ran even faster, calling the granite to me. The chunks and slabs swam up and swirled around me, shaping themselves into a protective shell.

When they were done, Mary Lou and I were encased in rubble, the only opening a narrow slit at eye level.

Bullets peppered our stone armor, pinging and zinging in all directions. Nothing could penetrate that granite hide, though.

"What the hell *is* that?" snapped Crystal, continuing to shoot. "Get *outta* there!"

My answer was to extend my mind beyond the shell, scoop up a pile of mud, and heave it at Crystal. She howled with rage as the mud splattered all over her, knocking her back a step and stopping the gunfire at least for a moment.

It was enough time for me to gather more mud and rocks and fling them at Crystal in another barrage. She fought to keep her feet and advanced through sheer force of will, bucking the tide of mud and stone.

Lightning flared and thunder boomed as I put the stone suit in motion. The legs of fused rubble bent at my command, marching me toward Crystal even as I pelted her with the hardest pebbles and shards of rock I could find.

"Give me the baby!" she shouted, cranking off a few last rounds as the storm of earth became too much for her. "She's mine!"

Not a chance. Lightning flashed as I hurled the biggest mass yet of stone and soil, this time blowing the rifle from Crystal's grip and driving her to her knees.

Stomping over, I pulled back one powerful arm of the stone suit and lashed out, splaying Crystal unconscious in the mud. Her still form was blasted by the rain, illuminated by the flickering glow of lightning.

Soon enough, red and blue lights flashed over her, too, coming from the direction of the road beyond the woods. I knew it meant a police cruiser had arrived, and I smiled.

My partner was about to join us.

I released the granite shell, letting it fall to pieces around me. By the time Sheriff Dale Briar appeared through the trees, I was standing amid the rubble with no protection from the pouring rain, cradling little Mary Lou in my arms.

"Look who I found." I smiled down at the wailing baby. "She's had quite an adventure."

"Great work, Gaia." Briar wasn't surprised that I took care of this single-handedly. As my boyfriend, he knows quite well what I can do when I put my Mother Earth mind to it. "What about the abductor?" He waved his rifle at Crystal, who was half-buried under mud and rock between us.

"She's fine." I reached out with one hand and channeled power through my fingers, moving the worst of the debris off Crystal's body.

Briar spotted her rifle a few yards away, sticking out of a big clump of muck, and grabbed it. "Charmer Investigations does it again. The bad guys can't *win* as long as we've got the *world* on our side."

Just then, cop car sirens screamed in the distance, racing nearer.

"The Staties are coming, and the F.B.I. won't be far behind." Briar leaned the rifles against a tree and proceeded to cuff Crystal, who was lying on her stomach. "You want to get your story straight with the baby?"

"She won't rat me out, will you, sweetie?" I tickled Mary Lou's chin, and she stopped crying. "You won't tell the State Police about the suit made of stone, will you?"

Briar grinned at me. "You're great with kids, Gaia. Maybe because you're Mother Earth and all that."

"Maybe so, but this one *stinks* right now." I held her out as if I wanted him to take her. "Seriously! Try being stuck in a stone shell with limited ventilation and *that* toxic diaper sometime."

The sirens closed in, and multiple flashing lights splashed the woods where we stood. Briar tromped through the muck to give me a quick kiss, his nose wrinkling at the stench of the loaded diaper.

"You weren't kidding!" He waved at the fumes but took the child from me anyway.

Car doors opened, and cop boots scuffed on gravel. The Staties would be here at any moment.

Heart pounding, I stole a kiss from him. There was no denying we made a great team.

So what if one of us is the human avatar of an entire planet, equipped with powers beyond those of any normal mortal woman or man? At least he could say I was his whole *world* and totally mean it, right?

"Are you sure you don't want me to make myself scarce?" I asked. "This is the third time in a month I've helped with a case. What if they start saying you can't solve a crime without your girlfriend?"

"They already say that." Briar grinned and rocked the baby in his arms. "And guess how many shits I give?"

"None?"

He laughed. "As long as the bad guys get caught, I'm happy. I couldn't be *prouder* that it's *you* doing the catching."

"Thanks, honey." I smiled and straightened as the Staties pushed closer through the brush. "The feeling's mutual."

"I love you, Gaia Charmer." Briar winked and walked with the baby toward the onrushing Staties.

Watching him go, I experienced a rush of strong emotion. We'd been seeing each other for six months, ever since we'd worked together to defeat the Groundswell organization and the dark being behind it, Atlantis (the guiding force of the ancient sunken continent).

My relationship with Briar had kept me balanced in the wake of Groundswell, which had been a difficult time for me. It isn't every day you find out you're not just a private eye with the power to control rock and stone—you're the personification of *Mother Earth* herself.

Being with Briar had kept me happy all those months, had enabled me to keep on living a normal life in spite of the revelations about my true nature. Being with him fulfilled me—though it was true, I sometimes felt guilty for not exploring my Mother Earth heritage more. As the walking heart and soul of the world, I probably should have been fighting climate change or something...but there would be time for that later, I kept telling myself.

Never mind that one friend in particular—Phaola, a nymph who'd helped me fight Groundswell and gone on to become the Landkind known as the Lady of the Alleghenies—had called bullshit on my attitude. More than once, she'd pushed me to step up and make more of an effort to fulfill my duties as Mother Earth. *They're killing you,* she'd said. *Stop pretending you're one of them.*

Phaola's words went in one ear and out the other. Whatever my connection to the Earth, I felt *totally* human and driven by my heart.

"Hold your fire," Briar told the Staties. "The hostage is safe, and the suspect is secure."

The rain was finally slowing as Briar and the three state cops talked. It had mostly let up by the time the two F.B.I. agents got there.

"Gaia, this is Agent Frank Wagner." Briar gestured at the shorter of the two, a dark-haired man in his forties or so with a grim smile on his hollow-cheeked face. "I've known him a long time."

"Good to meet you, Gaia." Frank's handshake was firm and steady. "Dale's told me a lot about you."

His partner, a fit young woman with long, blonde hair, stepped in with a handshake of her own. "Agent Judy Lewis," she said. "And you're some kind of law enforcement, I take it?"

"Consulting detective," I told her.

"Gaia *should* be on the force," said Briar. "She's that good. She's the one who brought down the abductor and saved the child."

"In that case, well done." Frank gave her a little bow. "If you're good enough to save a life and stop a menace to society, you're good enough for me."

Judy frowned. "You did all that yourself?" She looked around at the rubble and disrupted muck with Crystal's inert form in the middle of it.

"I had a little help, actually," I told her. "Crystal kept making stupid-ass mistakes."

Frank chuckled. "Well, Briar here better watch out. Judy and I might just have to recruit you ourselves! We're always looking for people like you."

"I might just consider an offer like that," I said. "Unless a certain *sheriff* I know finally gives me a *pay raise.*"

"God knows you deserve it." Briar smiled. "But your hourly rate is *already* higher than what they pay *me!*"

Everyone laughed. Mary Lou wailed as if she had something of her own to say, and they all laughed harder.

That was pretty much the end of the fun. As the laughter faded, paramedics raced to the scene in an ambulance and whisked away Mary Lou to give her a thorough exam. That left me to move on to the next phase of the evening's entertainment—telling the F.B.I. and State Police my version of the facts.

It felt like I did it at least a dozen times, going over everything that had happened—leaving out the dirt and rock manipulation, of course. I didn't talk about the stone suit, either, or anything else that might have given away my secrets. To hear me tell it, my apprehension of Crystal had been strictly a manual takedown, a triumph of physical strength and endurance on my part.

I spun a good yarn, I thought, and got through it without arousing suspicion about my extra earthiness...but the questioning still took a toll on my mood. By the time we were done, I was no longer the chipper self who'd joked around mere moments ago. My mood had taken a decidedly dark turn.

Not that such a turn was at all uncommon for me. Have I mentioned I'm bipolar? I know, it figures. And I try to take away the moods' power over me by giving them silly nicknames.

Let's just say the mood I was in just then was more like "Sinking Fast" than "Smooth Sailing."

3

The next morning was sunny and warm in downtown Confluence, Pennsylvania as I walked into the office where I ran my two businesses—Charmer Investigations and Cruel World Travel. As I entered in my brown leather jacket, black jeans, and scoop-neck white top, the chime on the door played a few bars of the classic song "Caravan," just like always.

It wasn't a song I'd picked. The blame for that belonged to my partner, Duke, who looked back at me over the local newspaper from one of the three desks occupying the front room. Duke's the one who *wrote* that song, in a way, since he's a golem, a creature of the Earth possessed by the spirit of a certain famous bandleader with the last name Ellington.

I don't keep him around for his musical skills, though. He's my *moon*–a helper who keeps me from spinning out of control. There's nobody in the world who knows me better, not even Briar—nobody who can *manage* me better.

Not to mention, he makes the best coffee *anywhere*...though for once, he didn't have a cup waiting when I strolled in.

That instantly put me on edge. "What's wrong with this picture?" Scowling, I marched over to my desk, picked up the empty mug there (the one with a cartoon image of the Earth on its face, grinning and giving a thumbs-up sign) and turned it upside-down. Nothing came out.

Duke shrugged. "You'll have to talk to the new girl about that, Earth Angel." He turned a page of the newspaper and continued reading through his gold-rimmed spectacles. "Coffee-making is no longer my bag."

"New girl?" He and I were alone in the room. "What new girl?"

"Hello."

At the sound of the stranger's voice, I whirled to see a young woman emerge from the doorway leading to the back room. She was short and stocky, with pale gray eyes and platinum hair that fell in a springy bob to her shoulders. Even dressed casually in a gray-and-white sweater and black jeans, she had a striking look.

"What's going on here?" For the moment, I ignored the girl and spoke only to Duke. "What *exactly* is this all about?"

Duke pointed at the side of his head. "My sanity, that's what. And our success."

"Very good to meet you, Ms. Charmer." The new girl extended a hand.

I stuck out a single upraised index finger, putting her off. "Duke, I am *not* in a great mood this morning..."

Duke smirked. "Now *there's* a surprise."

"...so how about cutting the crap? What's the *story?*"

"You've been making headlines." Duke held up the newspaper, which had a photo of me with the rescued baby on the front page. "As a result of the positive publicity, people want to do business with you more than ever. That's wonderful, yes? But not so much for your poor *partner*, good Sir Duke...especially since you've been out running around getting that fine *publicity* all the time."

"It's paid work," I said. "Would you rather I *didn't* take cases and just focused on the travel agency?"

"That's not what I said or meant, my dear," said Duke. "The simple fact is, while you've been taking care of the field work, I've been left to handle everything else—and it has gotten the better of me. I know I *look* young..." He didn't, really; he looked like he was 75, which had been his age on the day he died. "...but I am no longer in my prime in some ways. Realizing I desperately needed help, I prepared to run an ad in the local paper—but before I could place the order, *this* flower of efficiency walked through the door, looking for work."

When I glanced back at the new girl, she nodded enthusiastically.

"I daresay, it was the beginning of a beautiful friendship." Duke chuckled. "And now, if you'll allow me to make the introductions? Gaia, meet Luna. Luna, meet Gaia."

"Great to meet you, Gaia," she said, again sticking out her hand.

Instead of shaking it, I turned my full attention on Duke. "As partners, I thought we had to agree on all major decisions, including hires."

"To be honest, Earth Angel," he said, lowering his voice, "it was *this,* or you'd be looking for a new *partner.* And a *new moon,* as well."

I didn't have anything to say to that. The truth was, I'd had no idea that Duke was struggling. As usual, he'd soldiered on without complaining...though now I found myself wondering if there'd been signs all along and I'd missed them.

It was possible. I'd been pretty preoccupied lately, trying to figure out my life and all.

"Okay then." Turning, I extended a hand to Luna. "Nice to meet you, Luna. Welcome aboard."

Luna looked relieved as she accepted the handshake. "Thank you, Ms. Charmer."

"Gaia." I noticed her hand was cool and dry to the touch. She looked like she was in her early twenties, just a few years younger than I was. A few years younger than my current human form, I should say. "Call me Gaia."

"Thank you, Gaia." As she met my gaze, she did more than smile—she *beamed.* Her expression, in contrast to her chilly touch, was overflowing with warmth. "I'll try my best not to let you down."

Her apparent sincerity made me feel a bit better about bringing in a complete stranger to work in the office. I'd been burned before and learned to be suspicious of those I hadn't vetted to the hilt...but maybe this one would be okay. Duke liked her well enough, after all, and he was great at judging character.

Even as our handshake broke apart, I resolved to give her a chance and hope for the best. If she could take some of the pressure off Duke and keep him happy, she'd be worth every penny of her paycheck and then some.

"Now that that's settled," I said, crossing the office to my personal desk, "could *somebody* get me some damn *coffee?*"

Luna scooted over, grabbed my empty mug, and smiled. "Double cream, double sugar." She nodded. "Duke told me how you like it."

"Good old Duke." I shot him a look. "Always thinking of his partner."

"I can't imagine doing otherwise." Duke nodded sagely, a twinkle in his eye.

"Okay then." I shrugged out of my leather jacket, slung it over the back of my chair, and sat down. "What's on our agenda for this morning?"

"Don't ask me." Duke raised the newspaper so I couldn't see his face. "Luna's running your schedule now."

"By the way, you have a client meeting in five minutes," said Luna as she darted out of the back with my coffee.

I shook my head with annoyance. "Are you sure you couldn't've waited a little *longer* to tell me about it?"

"Sorry about that." Luna put the steaming mug on the desk in front of me. "First day on the job, y'know."

"Which side of the business is the meeting about?" I asked. "Detective agency or travel?"

"*Both,*" said Duke from behind the newspaper. "The meeting is about both."

"You knew about it, too?" I said.

"Of course." Duke winked at me over the newspaper. "I'm the one who set it up."

Just as he said it, the front door opened, and the chime played "Caravan." A tall, dark-skinned woman in a flowing yellow dress and spiky gold heels entered the room. She was slim and graceful, with dark eyes and close-cropped black hair that perfectly framed her elegant features. She was *so* beautiful, in fact, that she forced us all to take note; she had a bearing that I could best describe as regal.

"Hello." Luna hurried over and shook her hand. "I'm Luna Neil. We spoke on the phone."

"Very good to meet you." The woman's accent was hard to place. I wasn't sure if she'd picked it up in Eastern Europe, Africa, or India.

"Gaia Charmer, this is Ashanti Moneta," said Luna. "She's your ten o'clock."

I got to my feet and shook Ashanti's hand. "My pleasure, Ashanti. And this..." I gestured at the man behind the newspaper. "...is my partner, Duke."

Duke rattled the paper but didn't emerge from behind it. "Welcome to our most humble abode, Ashanti."

I gestured for her to take a seat, and then I sat down across from her at my desk. "So what can we help you with today?"

"I want to take a trip," said Ashanti, her gold hoop earrings jiggling as she spoke. "I want to return to my long-lost *selfland*."

"Your what?" I asked. "Do you mean your homeland?"

She shook her head insistently. "I meant what I said. My *selfland*, as in the *land* that is my *self*." She lowered her eyes. "Or *was*, anyway."

I played with my pleated braid as I sometimes did when things got interesting. "You were one with the land? Is that what you're saying?"

"I *was* the land." Her expression turned fierce. "And then I was taken away from it. The land was *stolen* from me, and I was sent *very* far away."

Duke lowered his newspaper, suddenly engaged. "Where *is* this selfland, exactly?"

"That's just it." Her eyes glistened with tears. "I don't *know*."

I watched her closely, trying to gauge her sincerity and veracity. Since my time six months ago at Parapets—the high-tech research base where the monsters of Groundswell had tried to end humanity —there'd been more people around who knew I was unique. I had to stay on the lookout for folks looking to take advantage of me to further their bad intentions as Groundswell had done.

"Please, you've got to help me," said Ashanti. "The Lady of the Alleghenies said you could. She said you were a friend to all Landkind...whatever *Landkind* is."

Looking askance, I saw Luna leaning on a desk, listening with keen attention. I'd been hoping to keep her in the dark about my secrets, but that option was off the table now...unless I bluffed, accused Ashanti of being a nut, and threw her out.

But if she *was* Landkind, I could never do that. It was true I'd let my Mother Earth duties slide while enjoying my romance with Briar, but turning my back on *family* was one thing I'd *never* do.

As an avatar of one of Earth's many landforms—a mountain, valley, river, island, etc. in human form—she *was* family to me. In a way, she was *part* of me.

If she was really Landkind.

"The Lady of the Alleghenies sent you?" I asked.

Ashanti nodded. "Phaola herself. She sends her regards, Miss Glow. She asks that you do whatever you can to restore my rightful place in the world."

I still felt leery, I couldn't help it...but I decided I couldn't turn my back on her. Not yet, anyway.

"All right." I would go down this road with her a little ways, at least. "Let's give this a try."

Suddenly, Ashanti lit up. "You'll take me back there? To my selfland?"

"I can't make any promises," I told her, "but I'll see what I can do."

"Oh, thank you!" said Ashanti. "I can never thank you enough for giving me hope, Miss Glow!"

I frowned. "Why do you keep calling me 'Miss Glow?' You know that's not my name, right?"

"It just seems *right*," said Ashanti. "You *definitely* have a *glow* about you."

As odd as her rationale seemed, I decided not to press her further on the matter...for now. "How will you pay my fee?"

Ashanti leaned forward, folding her hands on the desk, and closed her eyes. Her expression became a frown, and the frown deepened; her head lowered, and her body shook.

Little gasps escaped her lips as if she were undergoing tremendous strain. Her hands tightened, her fingers clenching so hard her knuckles whitened.

Then, suddenly, she let out one last gasp and relaxed. The shaking stopped, and she leaned back in the chair.

Her eyes fluttered open. Her hands unfolded, revealing an object on the desk that they had hidden until now.

A huge gem glittered on the rubbery black surface, big as a robin's egg, brighter and more crystal clear than an icicle in the sun.

"Will this cover it?" Ashanti held out the gem to me. "If not, I'll summon another one."

"I thought *I* was the only one who knew tricks like that." Duke whistled appreciatively and ran a hand over his wavy black hair. "Yet you've done me one better, Ms. Moneta. *Gold bars* are the best *I've* ever managed to manifest. Now here you've gone and summoned up a lovely *diamond.*"

Ashanti gazed thoughtfully at the jewel in her palm. "Sometimes I wonder if these are clues to where I came from."

Duke plucked the diamond from her hand and held it up to the light. "I do believe you're playing my tune, Ms. Moneta. What about you, Earth Angel?"

"I think you should lock that up somewhere safe." I got up from my desk and pulled on my jacket. "Then you and I should go for a walk," I told Ashanti.

"Where?" she asked.

"Caravan" played as I tugged the door open. "Somewhere without so much interference," I said, shooting Duke and Luna a look. "A place where the *reception* is better."

4

I didn't have to drive far to get to the woods—one of the advantages of living in a small town like Confluence. Less than fifteen minutes after pulling away from the office in my black hybrid Toyota Highlander SUV, I was rolling up the road into Smoke Ring Lake State Park.

Already, I was feeling better about my day. Something I'd learned since discovering my true nature was that the further I got from human development, the more my mood improved. Even a small town like Confluence was enough to make me tense; being away from buildings and closer to trees, bodies of water, and, yes, *earth*, always gave me a lift.

It made total sense. Being an avatar of the planet, of course I'd feel at my best when there was nothing coming between me and the planet.

"Here we are." I pulled into a parking area near the lake and switched off the Highlander. "Time for that walk I promised."

Ashanti got out of the Highlander and looked around. "Why here in particular?"

I got out, too, and shut my door. "It's a good place to clear my head. Fresh air helps me think."

"I see." Ashanti shut the door on the passenger side and followed me onto a nearby path through the trees. "Perhaps you are also hoping this place might spur some memories, Miss Glow?"

"Hey, that's not a bad idea." I nodded. "Let me know if anything jumps out at you, okay?"

As we continued down the path, the sound of twittering birds and chirping chipmunks filled the air. The world spoke to me as it always did, in shafts of sunlight, fluttering leaves, gentle breezes—and so much more besides. I sensed it all around me at once, from the vast blue skies far above to the tiniest quivering particles of matter on the subatomic level. There were worlds within worlds in the Earth, all of them moving and singing and changing—all of them, in their own way, part of me, an extension of my substance and awareness.

We emerged from the path at the top of a green, grassy bank leading down to the lake. In two weeks, when the park opened for swimmers, it would be a very different scene, one I knew quite well given my contact with local lands and waters. The bank would be crowded from end to end with sunbathers on towels and blankets, unleashed at last to greedily soak up the warmth and sunshine. There would be kids and dogs running, frisbees and footballs flying, people of all ages shouting and laughing and splashing in the water with manic glee. Summer-worshipping folks would swarm the park, competing to make up for too many months of grueling winter and waterlogged spring in this part of the country. The Earth would respond to their touch, I knew, all too happy to cast off the snow and muck and loneliness in return for the joyful press of bodies and the song of so many voices upraised in praise of warm weather and simple pleasures.

"What do you think of this place?" I asked. "Does it remind you of anything?"

Ashanti frowned. "I have no special feelings about it."

"No déjà vu, huh?"

Ashanti shook her head, then turned a suspicious look in my direction. "You don't think *this* is my selfland, do you?"

I shrugged. "I don't know *what* I think yet." Then I started walking toward the water's edge. "So tell me, Ashanti. What *do* you remember?"

She stayed beside me, looking regal as ever. "Not much, I'm afraid." The breeze rippled her bright yellow dress and batted her gold hoop earrings. "I remember meeting the Lady of the Alleghenies, and her telling me to seek you out. I remember calling your office and making an appointment, and then I walked in and met you and your staff."

"But what do you remember about your past before that?" I asked. "The people or landforms you knew?"

Ashanti sighed heavily. "Nothing."

"Your memory's a blank?"

"Not a *complete* blank," said Ashanti. "It's more like...*impressions* in the fog. I *know* things, but I don't *remember* them. I can't make out the *details.*"

"Like you were born yesterday," I said.

She nodded. "Yes, exactly."

I understood better than she knew. Not so long ago, I'd been reborn in my current body without any memories of the multitude of past lives I'd lived as the Earth's human avatar—amnesia caused by Atlantis as punishment for sinking his kingdom eons ago. Duke, created by my previous self, had been my saving grace; without a guide like him, extreme memory loss would have been hell to go through.

"Tell me about these impressions." I stopped at the edge of the lake and turned to her. "Focus on them the best you can and describe anything that comes to you."

Ashanti closed her eyes. She remained silent for long moments, her brows knit in concentration.

"Warmth," she said at last. "Warmth and light and company. Togetherness."

I watched her and didn't interrupt. I worried that if I stopped the flow of memory now, it might never restart.

"Hmm." She tilted her head to one side. "Sudden change. Disruption. *Pain.*" She bit her lip. "Then...falling. *Impact.*" She paused. "Nothingness."

So focused was I on her words, I didn't notice the shadow drifting over the lake. I didn't pay attention to the patch of darkness moving toward us, projected by the cluster of clouds drifting high over the water.

"So much nothingness," said Ashanti. "Then, suddenly...*light. Thought. Sadness.* The smell of...*damp* and *must* and *oil.* The sound of *men* and *machines.* Shaking and rumbling *everywhere.* And then...and then..." She opened her eyes. "And then, your office...and this."

I played with my braid, taking in everything she'd said. "What else?"

Ashanti pursed her lips and looked off to the side. "*Nothing* else. Nothing I can remember."

All told, she hadn't given me much, and I was disappointed. "Are you sure? Relax and think back."

"Well..." She looked up then, and her eyes shot wide open. Her demeanor shifted suddenly, swinging from deep concentration to extreme agitation. "Look out!"

Before I could react in any way, a bright flash lit the sky. Even as I turned, a blast of flame sizzled down and seared the ground between us.

Leaping into action, I focused on the layer of pebbles under the surface of the fringe of the lake and lifted up as many as I could with my power. A mass of them broke the surface of the water and hung there, draining and awaiting my direction.

Before I could make them take flight, another plume of fire slashed down from above, coming close enough that I could feel its intense heat on my skin. The shock of it knocked me off balance, and I stumbled, releasing my hold on the rocks. They dropped back into the water with a loud splash.

Ashanti caught my elbow and helped me steady myself, even as another fiery blast surged toward us. I threw myself against her, tackling her to the ground just as the fire licked through the place where we'd just been standing.

"You need to run for it!" I told her. "Whatever this thing is, I'll take care of it!" Even as I said it, I was reaching out with my power, digging into the layer of pebbles again. This time, I'd launch them rapid-fire at the cloud, firing them like bullets instead of gathering and heaving them all at once.

"You'll be burned alive!" shouted Ashanti.

"Go!" Looking up, I saw the fire jet had burned away some of the cottony material from the front of the cloud, exposing the tip of what looked like some kind of dark snout. I squinted, trying to make out more detail.

That was when Ashanti suddenly leaped to her feet and threw

her arms in the air. "No!" Her head fell back and her body shimmered with rippling golden light, swiftly growing in intensity.

"Ashanti?" Gazing at her, I briefly forgot the flames. Whatever transformation she was going through, it suggested reserves of incredible power welling within her, power I hadn't expected.

Without a word, she swung her arms forward, aiming at the cloud. The aura of light seething around her flared so bright, I had to shield my eyes. The light churned and flowed, rushing up to form a blazing orb of light around her hands, a sun in miniature.

Then, she cried out, and the orb pulsed into the sky. It flashed up just as another jet of flame was pouring forth and engulfed the cloud in a blinding burst of energy.

The cloud and whatever it held exploded with a thunderous boom and a massive flare that hung in the sky like the biggest billowing shell of a fireworks show finale.

With a gasp, Ashanti dropped her arms and slumped. The energy flowing around her faded suddenly, leaving her standing there as if she hadn't changed at all a moment ago.

Then, her legs buckled, and she fell. I caught her and held her in my arms, staring at her face as ash drifted around us like feathery black snow.

"What was *that* all about?" I asked. "Who the hell are you *really*, Ashanti Moneta?"

My only answer was the ash sailing down, bits of it clinging to her sleeping, regal features.

5

"She can generate and project energy blasts? Is *that* all?" Briar stared at Ashanti as two paramedics worked on her on a gurney behind the ambulance, which was parked near Smoke Ring Lake. "I thought you said there was something *special* about her, Gaia."

I stood with him near the foot of the gurney, arms folded over my chest. "I know, right? Sorry I got your hopes up." The paramedics had said she'd be fine, but I was still worried. Ashanti's transformation had seemed to take a lot out of her.

Her pulse had been so weak and thready, I'd acted fast to bring in help. I'd dialed 9-1-1 right after her collapse, then called Briar. Whatever Ashanti's secrets might be, looping him in could help me find answers.

He already had a CSI gathering ash and other evidence for analysis, and he'd started circulating a photo of Ashanti in search of identification. Briar was an awesome cop; he was great at his job, possessed a good heart, and had access to law enforcement resources I couldn't otherwise tap.

"I guess I'll leave the fire-breathing cloud out of my report for now," he said, stepping back and lowering his voice so the paramedics couldn't hear. "And, y'know...the energy blasts from her fingertips."

"Sounds like a plan," I told him. "Or you could always go with a freak lightning strike. That would fit with the scorch marks on the ground, right?"

He flattened his hand and waggled it with fingers spread. "Eh, maybe."

I turned my gaze back to Ashanti on the gurney. "Well, it's not like the police report's our main concern right now, is it?"

"Agreed," said Briar, still keeping his voice low. "I, for one, am *much* more interested in finding out who the hell tried to kill *you* out here today."

"You and me both, Sheriff." As I said it, Ashanti woke with a start, a sharp inhalation of breath. There was a flurry of action as the paramedics responded to her revival, checking her thoroughly—and then they raised the head of the gurney, bringing her to a seated position.

Her face lit up when she saw me smiling back at her from the foot of the gurney. "Miss Glow! I'm so glad you're all right!"

"Ditto," I said. "And I'm glad *you're* all right, too."

Ashanti laughed. To me, she looked and sounded as if she hadn't been through anything more eventful than a peaceful walk along Smoke Ring Lake. "Aren't you going to introduce me to your friend?"

"I guess so." I sighed overdramatically. "If I have to."

Ashanti patted the bedding on the gurney. "Only if you want the patient to feel better."

She seemed to be feeling just fine, I thought—better than before, actually, as if the power surge had left her energized somehow. "Ashanti Moneta, meet Sheriff Dale Briar. Sheriff Briar, this is Ashanti."

"Very good to meet you, Ms. Moneta." Briar smiled and tipped his hat. "I'm only sorry the circumstances couldn't be better ones."

"I'm fine," said Ashanti. "Other than the complete memory loss, that is."

The paramedics made a few last checks, since she'd declined to let them take her to the hospital, then helped her down from the gurney and went to work packing their gear. Ashanti walked over to us on steady legs, straightening her yellow dress, which had gotten wrinkled.

"So." I gestured in the general direction of the lake. "Any idea what happened with the fire-breathing cloud?"

She shook her head. "I was hoping *you* could tell *me.*"

"Has anyone ever tried to kill you before?" I asked. "That you can remember?"

"No," said Ashanti. "How about you?"

I didn't answer, though the answer was "way too often." Surviving murder attempts was part of my job...and part of my personal life, at least ever since my true history came to light six months ago.

"How do you know they weren't coming after *you* instead of *me?*" asked Ashanti.

"I guess I don't," I said. "But that *was* the first time I was ever attacked out here by a fire-breathing cloud thing...and I was with you."

"Good point," said Ashanti.

"So has anything come back to you since the fight?" I asked. "Any clear memories of your life?"

She thought a moment, then shrugged. "Sorry, no."

"Okay." I watched her face closely. "But do you *feel* any different? I mean, you *collapsed* after you fired those energy beams."

Ashanti frowned. "Did I really collapse? I don't remember."

"You did," I told her. "You lit up with energy and shot off a bolt that blew up whatever was in that cloud. Then you just passed out on the ground."

"That's crazy," said Ashanti.

"Maybe the energy blast just took a lot out of you," I suggested. "It was too much strain."

Ashanti's frown deepened. "Is that what happened to you, too? Did your power take a lot out of you?"

Just then, Briar's phone rang, and he stepped away to answer it. At that point, it was just Ashanti and I standing there together in the springtime breeze and sunlight, face to face.

It was then that she turned her hands around to take hold of mine. "I remember seeing the stones lift out of the lake, and it seemed like you were making it happen. You were so *focused.* And then the fire broke your concentration, and they all *fell.*"

I didn't answer. She was still such an unknown quantity, I was hesitant to trust her. It meant a lot that Phaola had vouched for her; Phaola and I had been through hell together, and over the past months, we'd come through it as the best of friends. She'd gone down the wrong path for a while but changed course and helped me save all humanity. In the end, as I'd come into my power as Mother Earth's avatar, I'd appointed her the new Lady of the Alleghenies, replacing the previous one, Laurel, who'd perished. So Phaola's word carried a lot of weight with me.

Ashanti's voice lowered almost to a whisper. "Are you Landkind yourself, Miss Glow? Is that why you have powers? Is that why the Lady of the Alleghenies sent me to you?"

I felt the urge to tell her who I was—but not yet. I still needed to know more about her first. I needed to make sure Phaola hadn't been deceived, and Ashanti had not been sent to harm me or people I cared about.

"Ashanti," I said, choosing my words carefully. "All you need to know is, I want to help. I will do everything I can to get you back to your rightful place."

"Please tell me who you really are, Gaia," she pressed, squeezing my hands harder.

Before either of us could say another word, Briar hurried over with phone in hand. "I have to go." His voice and expression were grim. "Gaia, I'll talk to you later."

"Okay." I didn't ask for more details in front of a civilian I wasn't sure we could trust. "Good luck, rock hound." It was a nickname, since Briar was a rock collector and amateur gemologist.

He was already on the phone with his next call, jogging toward his cruiser. The best he managed was a thumbs-up over his shoulder on the run.

Leaving me to wonder what the hell he'd been called away so urgently for, and to worry about his well-being when he got in the middle of it.

6

"Where to now?" asked Ashanti as we rolled back into town in the Highlander. "Someplace without killer clouds, I hope."

"You're *half* right." I drove a little further, then pulled into the parking lot of the newest shop on Main Street. The name of the place, scrolled in green and white on the front window, was *Scintillas in the Mist.*

As soon as we walked in the door, the owners spun and greeted us, beaming with sheer delight. "Gaia!" they both shouted at the same time, their elation obvious.

"Minthe and Nephelae, I'd like you to meet Ashanti," I said. "Ashanti, these are my good friends Minthe and Nephelae."

"Nice to meet you." Ashanti nodded.

"Any friend of Gaia's..." said Minthe.

"...is *competition* for us!" finished Nephelae.

The two of them giggled excitedly. Life in the mortal world—and Confluence in particular—never seemed to get old for them. You might feel that way too if you'd been freed to live life as you choose after spending millennia as nymphs cursed to never leave certain magical places.

"You're both in luck today! We're having a 50% off sale!" Minthe, a brunette with deep green highlights, had been trapped in a field of mint for most of her life. She didn't look a day over twenty-one, but her true age was in the thousands of years.

Nephelae, who had platinum blonde hair with light blue high-lights, looked just as young...and was every bit as old. "Every customer is eligible for a complimentary cup of green matcha tea," she told us. "Come have a seat while Minthe fixes it."

Nephelae gestured at one of the little wrought iron tables with two white wicker chairs in the front section of the shop, and Ashanti and I sat. The nymphs made most of their money selling herbs, incense, candles, and aromatherapy compounds, but they also had a nice sideline serving teas and select goodies in the shop's café area.

"So what brings you here today?" asked Minthe. "Doing a little shopping for Sheriff Briar?"

She and Nephelae giggled, even as Ashanti turned a funny look my way.

"Are you here to talk about our next trip?" asked Nephelae. "We're still torn between the Galapagos and the Tianzi Mountains of China."

"Though we're open to other ideas, if you know of something *extra*-special," added Minthe.

"Actually, I was hoping you could help us with something," I said.

"Anything, anytime, anywhere, girlfriend," said Minthe.

"Gaia helped us out in a big way a while back," Nephelae explained to Ashanti. "We owe her more than we can ever repay."

"I was their travel agent," I told Ashanti. "I did some special bookings for them, that's all."

It was an understatement, but I was still playing certain cards close to my vest. It was true that Minthe and Nephelae had been customers of Cruel World Travel...but the help I'd provided, at least at first, had been to free them from the bonds that had locked them down for so many ages. Thanks to me (after a harrowing battle with a coven of ancient witches) they'd gone on to travel the world...and, eventually, settled in Confluence and started a business. In the months since the collapse of Parapets—an event I'd been drawn into after the death of my best friend, Aggie—they'd become even closer friends and confidants of mine.

"So what kind of help do you need, exactly?" asked Minthe.

"Ashanti and I were just attacked out at Smoke Ring Lake. It was some kind of fire-breathing cloud thing. I was hoping you could tell us more about it."

"You've come to the right place." If anyone could tell me what I needed to know, it was Nephelae. After all, she had a special affinity for clouds after being *trapped* in one since the time of the ancient Greeks. "It breathed *fire*, you say? Not lightning?"

"That's right," I said. "Big blasts of flame like something out of a dragon's maw. I caught a glimpse of what looked like a dark snout, but it could've been just about anything."

"Wow." Nephelae folded her arms over her chest and tapped her chin with an index finger. "I don't think I've *ever* seen anything like that, Gaia."

"What about..." I glanced at Ashanti, wondering if I should ask her to step away before my next question—then decided to let the chips fall where they may. "What about any gods or creatures you might have encountered?"

Ashanti's eyes widened, but she said nothing.

"Hmm." Nephelae closed her eyes and rocked back and forth on the balls of her feet, deep in thought. "Zeus threw lightning bolts, but I don't remember him hiding behind clouds to do it. Fire was more up Hephaestus' alley, but he wasn't an airborne type at all." She thought some more, then opened her eyes. "Prometheus *stole* fire from the gods, but he didn't fly, either."

"This was definitely an airborne attacker," I said.

Nephelae frowned. "You're *sure* it wasn't a dragon?"

"I'm sure." Just then, Minthe brought my steaming cup of matcha and put it on the table in front of me. "What about a fire sprite or elemental?" I asked.

"It's possible," said Nephelae, "though I haven't seen one in ages. Climate change has been rough on them, you know."

"A demon, maybe? Or an ifrit?" suggested Minthe.

Nephelae nodded. "Either of those makes sense."

"It does?" Ashanti looked confused. "But there's no such *thing* as gods and dragons and demons, *is* there?"

"Poor thing." Minthe looked at her sadly.

"Have you been living under a rock or something?" said Nephelae.

Minthe sighed. "But it doesn't matter anyway, I guess. We can't be more specific without some kind of evidence."

"What about this?" Ashanti pointed at a few dark flecks on the yellow sleeve of her dress. "Some of the ash stuck to me when the cloud-thing exploded."

"Can't hurt to take a closer look." Minthe left the room, then returned with a cotton swab and plastic baggie. She dabbed Ashanti's dress with the swab, picking up enough flecks of ash to darken the tip. "We can run a few spells over it and see if anything pops." She dropped the swab in the baggie and sealed it.

"We'd appreciate it," I said, sipping my tea. "The sooner we find out who or what was behind the attack, the better. Ashanti's in danger, and it doesn't help that she's lost her memory."

"You poor thing!" said Nephelae. "No *wonder* you've forgotten all about the fantastical side of reality!"

"When do you think you might be done examining the ash?" I asked.

"How about tomorrow?" asked Minthe. "We'll give you a call when we're ready."

"Deal." I finished my tea and stood. "Maybe you could put out some feelers in the meantime, too. Ask around a little about the fire-breathing cloud."

"Will do, Gaia," said Minthe.

"We'll ask around our peeps," said Nephelae. "*Discreetly,* of course."

"Just one more favor, guys," I told them. "Please be extra-careful and on the alert from here on out. Whoever tried to kill Ashanti, they might not like it that you're mixed up in this now."

"Sure, Gaia," said Nephelae.

"Don't worry about us." Minthe made a muscle with her bicep and growled. "We're all about the old-school hardcore, yo."

I laughed, because the attitude didn't fit the cute little brunette with the chirpy voice and ancient origins. The effects of her new infatuation with rap music had a way of popping up when I least expected.

"Good to know," I said. "But please don't hesitate to call if things go sideways, okay? Any time of day or night, understood?"

"Yeah, yeah," said Nephelae in her best put-upon teenager voice. "We promise we'll call, *Mother*."

It was more than a joke. Nephelae and Minthe both knew my true nature as the personification of Mother Earth and teased me about it from time to time...but the teasing was always done with love and respect.

"All right then." I smiled. "Give us a shout when you're ready. We're going for a drive in the meantime."

"We are?" Ashanti got up from her chair. "Where to?"

Just then, my phone pinged with a text from Briar. "Correction," I said. "Change of plans. We'll have to take that drive tomorrow morning."

"Why is that, Miss Glow?" asked Ashanti.

Heart racing, I texted Briar back. "Guys, can Ashanti hang out here with you for just a bit?"

"Sure," said Minthe.

"What's up?" asked Nephelae.

"There's been a murder," I said as I ran for the door. "And apparently, *Mother Earth* has taken credit for it!"

When I rolled up to the modest brick house in suburban Rich Township, I saw the crime scene was already crowded. In addition to Briar's cruiser, there were two Confluence P.D. cars, three State Police vehicles, an ambulance, and the medical examiner's van parked in the driveway and along the street. A van from the local TV station showed up, too, as I was walking around to the backyard...and I knew that was just the beginning.

I said hi to Marcus Greene, the uniform at the corner of the house, and he let me pass. I went straight to the part of the yard that was just off the patio; local cops and State Police were gathered there, huddled and looking down at something on the ground.

Briar must have heard or sensed my approach, because he looked up. "Gaia." He gestured for me to join him in the huddle.

Part of me didn't want to, because I knew what I'd see. Briar's texts had drawn me a picture, and it was awful.

But staying off to the side was not an option. Working with law enforcement when called to do so was my job...and this particular crime was personal.

I walked over, and Briar stepped back to make room for me. Looking down, I saw the murder victim's body on the ground, and my stomach churned...not because I wasn't used to seeing the aftermaths of atrocities like this.

But because it was the kind of murder that someone with my abilities might have been likely to commit.

The woman on the ground, Ellie Grenoble, was a local widow in her late seventies. I didn't know her well, but I'd seen her around town now and then. She'd even come to Cruel World Travel once or twice to pick up pamphlets for trips she was thinking about taking.

Now here she was, in her simple blue housedress, white sweater, and white sneakers, with her body so packed with dirt it was coming out of her mouth.

Dr. Renee Cox, the Medical Examiner, crouched by the body, dumping little scoops of the dirt from Ellie's mouth into a clear plastic vial. "It's like she was pumped full of dirt from some kind of high-pressure device. Palpating her lower body, I can feel lumps of the stuff as far down as her abdomen, pubis, and even her thighs."

"I don't *see* a high-pressure pump anywhere nearby," said the older of three Staties. His hair under the hat was bright white, and his nametag said *Sgt. Jeffreys.* "Anyone else?"

"She's just packed to the gills," said Renee, a middle-aged woman on the stocky side with curly brown hair. "Cause of death is most likely asphyxiation from all the dirt."

"But how did the dirt get *in* her?" asked Deputy Jim Withers, the young, blond Confluence cop who served as Briar's second in command.

"There *has* to be a pump around here." Another, younger Statie with jet black hair and dimples looked from one side to the other, hunting for traces of whatever machine had done the damage.

As for me, I didn't bother with that. I knew how possible it was to execute someone in just the same way with no special equipment whatsoever.

"Gaia." Briar led me away from the huddle around the body. "This is what the note I told you about looked like." He pulled out his phone and called up a photo for my benefit.

I stared at it, dumbfounded. I couldn't believe what I was seeing.

Mother Earth is coming for the wicked. That was what it said.

"I wouldn't exactly call Ellie Grenoble wicked," said Briar. "Would you?"

My heart hammered as I stared at the letter on his screen. "This is so wrong," I said, keeping my voice low. "Somebody's trying to frame me."

Briar spoke softly, too. "But hardly anyone knows who you really are."

"All it takes is one," I told him. "There were survivors at Parapets, you know. And Divinities. Some of them know the truth and might have a bone to pick."

"Still seems pretty extreme." Briar looked over his shoulder at the cops huddled around the dead body. "Did you detect anything when you were over there?"

I gave him an exasperated look. "I wasn't exactly *probing* the *crime scene*, Dale."

"Right, I know." He touched my arm. "But you *could*."

"While your guys and the state police watch me do my thing? Sounds like an awesome plan."

"I'll move them off, don't worry," said Briar. "They still need to go over the house and property. Renee will give you some space if I ask her, no worries."

I didn't like the idea. I didn't want to be anywhere near the spot where someone masquerading as me had murdered an innocent woman.

But I knew, if I wanted to find out who was behind this, I would have to get close. I would have to do everything in my power to find the answers I needed.

"Okay." I nodded. "Fine."

"Wait for my signal," said Briar, and then he marched back over to the huddle. Within moments, the gathered men had walked off to continue their work, leaving Briar and Renee alone with the body.

Briar waved for me to join them, and I did.

"Renee, would it be okay if Gaia took a look at Ellie's remains?" he asked.

"Sure." Renee took a sample of hair and dropped it in an evidence baggie. "I forgot one of my test kits in the van, anyway."

She handed me a pair of plastic gloves from the pocket of her jacket, and I put them on. Then, she got up and walked to the Medical Examiner's van parked out front, leaving Ellie's body in our custody for at least a moment or two.

I got down on my knees beside her, took a deep breath, and

went to work. Reaching out with my mind, I hunted for traces of the killer—anything that stood out as unusual.

The last flickers of human life were long gone by now, though the chemical reactions that continued in its wake were still in play. I sensed the external and internal bacteria turning against their host, breaking down her cells in one last orgiastic feast.

Moving deeper, I probed the molecular level, seeking anything that seemed out of place. There was nothing beyond the expected natural activity as Ellie's organic molecules disentangled, reverting to a state of entropy that would allow them to be absorbed and converted by the biosphere.

No clues were detectable in the tissues of Ellie's corpse—but maybe the non-organic contents of her body would shed a light on things. Renee wasn't back yet, and no cops other than Briar were around, so I decided to take a chance. Leaning closer, I took off one of the gloves and touched the dirt that had fallen from Ellie's mouth.

Immediately, I felt a quavering in my fingertips, a fizzing vibration that shot up my arm and into my head and chest. My vision rippled and flashed, and then my surroundings burst into something entirely different.

Suddenly, I was in a vast cavern of some kind, deep in the bowels of the world. Everywhere I looked, I saw roiling, flowing magma, glowing red and orange and yellow. It gave off unbearable heat, enough to burn away human flesh at the slightest touch.

And yet, I could have sworn I saw something moving within it, something *slithering* through the liquefied rock. It had to be an illusion, a molten vein that only *looked* like something living. *Nothing* alive could have possibly survived in that searing, superheated flow.

At least that's what I thought until a bubble came to the surface of the red-orange pool, then rose further slowly, revealing an unexpected form. As I watched, it became clear the rounded shape was no bubble at all, but the top of what looked like a human head. Up it slid, and I saw what seemed to be long, straight hair and a neck and shoulders, all of it made of the same crimson magma.

Then, suddenly, the head turned, and a glowing golden eye gazed at me from the steaming side of an all-too-feminine face. A face with a truly *wicked* expression etched into it, one that made my blood turn to ice.

Instinctively, I pulled away from Ellie...and the world around me changed back. The magma and woman were gone; I was out of the blistering cavern and back in the grass of a suburban backyard.

And Briar's hands were on my shoulders. "Are you all right? You cried out!"

"Yeah." I shook my head to clear it and got to my feet. "I'm fine."

"What did you see? A clue to the killer's identity?"

"I don't know," I told him, frowning. "I don't know *what* the hell I saw."

8

The pizza guy came around six o'clock that evening, bringing a large veggie pie to the offices of Cruel World Travel/Charmer Investigations. As upset as I was, I still had to eat, and Ashanti and Luna were hungry, too. Only Duke the golem had no appetite, since as a creature of animated dirt and rock, he didn't need to eat.

But Duke *did* look forward to playing his usual trick, trying to pay for the food with actual gold doubloon coins. It was a skill of his, drawing gold through his earthen substance from the depths of the world, and he loved using it to mess with people's expectations.

"My good man," he told the scrawny blond twentysomething pizza guy. "I assure you, these are *actual* gold doubloons from a treasure chest buried *deep* on an island off the coast of Yucatan, Mexico."

"I can only take cash," said the pizza guy.

"And that is exactly what these *are*," said Duke. "They are most assuredly *legal tender* of the Spanish Empire!"

"Cash only. *American* cash." The pizza guy hiked a thumb at his car idling on the street. "And I'm on the clock, know what I mean?"

Duke dropped a hand on the guy's shoulder and held up the three gold coins so the light glinted on them. "My friend, the *market* value of the gold alone is astronomical. The *historical* value is even *greater*. These fine coins, I daresay, are *priceless.*"

"That's what I thought. They aren't *worth* anything." The pizza guy broke away and stepped around Duke. "Could *somebody* please *pay* me in something other than *play money?*"

Duke sighed. "Have it your way, son. Luna, please provide him with the appropriate funds as requested."

Luna had already raided petty cash and handed over the money to the pizza guy. "Sorry about that," she told him. "There's a nice tip in there to make up for it."

The guy grinned at Luna. "No problem. Enjoy your dinner."

Then he left, shut the door, and all of us except Duke went to work on the pizza.

"Do you know how many times that young man has turned down my offer of an actual *fortune?*" Duke laughed. "I'd be willing to wager he'd do the very same thing if I tried to hand him a gold *ingot.*"

"That bit is getting old, Duke," I told him as I reached for a slice from the box.

"Strangely, I never tire of it." Duke chuckled and waved out the window as the pizza guy drove away. "I only regret that it didn't cheer you up a little, Earth Angel."

I took a bite of the pizza and chewed solemnly. I doubted there was *anything* that could cheer me up.

Could you blame me? Someone was out there, killing in my name, and they were still at large. So was whoever or whatever had tried to kill Ashanti and me at Smoke Ring Lake.

Talk about "one of those days." The mood I knew as "Sinking Fast" was at the controls and not going anywhere anytime soon.

"Miss Glow." Ashanti had a slice of pizza in her hand but wasn't eating it. "I understand if you can't take my case right now. You have a lot on your plate."

I didn't answer her at first. Handling her case while tracking down the Mother Earth killer might not be smart. But there was one possibility that kept me from bailing out on her.

"The cases might be connected," I said.

"They might?" asked Ashanti.

"I agree," said Duke, who was back in full-on serious mode. "It does seem like an awfully big coincidence that you and Ashanti were attacked by a murderous cloud on the *same day* that a local woman ended up murdered by someone using the 'Mother Earth' sobriquet."

"Or maybe they aren't connected at all," said Luna. "Maybe it's all a big coincidence."

I gave her a look, surprised she'd jumped in like that on day one of her job as an office assistant...but then I let go of the shock. Duke trusted her, and I trusted Duke without hesitation or limit. If he thought it was fine to bring Luna into our circle of trust, it was fine with me.

"I'm not dropping your case," I told Ashanti. "I can walk and chew gum at the same time," I told Duke.

"But can you *catch* a killer while *another* killer's trying to *murder* you and/or your *client?*" Duke shrugged. "You're pretty tough, Earth Angel, but can you honestly handle all *that?*"

I leaned on the edge of my desk and chewed another bite of pizza. Since discovering I was the planet Earth in human form, I thought I should be able to do pretty much anything. I ought to be able to tap into the power and wisdom of the entire world, after all, and use it to accomplish any task. I should finally be the master of my own self and life, discarding any limits that kept me from reaching my full potential.

Except that wasn't how it had worked out. I still seemed driven by the same weaknesses and insecurities as before. I still had the same problems I'd always had. It wasn't like someone had flipped a switch and turned me into a new person overnight.

So no, I wasn't honestly sure I could handle both cases without failing. But likewise, I knew in my heart that I couldn't and shouldn't give up on Ashanti in spite of the possible danger and distraction.

"I've handled worse than this," I reminded Duke.

"I can't argue with that," said Duke.

"Then don't. I've got it under control."

"Allow me to offer one last illustration, at least," said Duke. "I've had the pleasure of playing with some truly *magnificent* musicians in my time. Some, I considered gods among men, for all practical purposes. Yet even *they* on occasion let out a sour note. Even *they* had awful shows when everything went wrong. And *you*, my Earth

Angel..." His smile this time was wise, not mischievous. "...are one *magnificent* talent."

Just as he finished, the door swung open, and "Caravan" played on the chime.

"Evening." Sheriff Briar looked grim. "Are you having a meeting or something? I can come back later..."

"You're fine." I gestured at the remaining food on Luna's desk. "Help yourself to some pizza while you're here."

"No thanks." He shook his head. "I just thought I'd update you on Ellie."

My appetite was instantly gone. I dropped the half slice of pizza I had left in the trash can by my desk. "What did you find?"

"More dirt, all through the house," said Briar. "But *scattered,* not tracked. Just clumps of it all over the place...even the beds."

"The same kind of dirt that killed her?" I asked.

"Looks the same," said Briar. "But we won't know for sure until the lab compares the samples."

I nodded. "What else?"

"Not much," said Briar. "No visible footprints or other trace evidence, though our team isn't done going over the place yet. Whoever was there...it's like they weren't there at all."

"Any trace on the letter?" I asked.

"The lab hasn't found anything yet, but they're going over it again," said Briar. "No trace on the body either...except the dirt, of course."

"Perhaps things will take a positive turn in the hours to come," said Duke. "The key evidence might yet reveal itself, Sheriff."

"I hope you're right." Briar cast a look at the pizza, then shook his head and turned away. "But we're not having much luck with the attack at the lake, either. Whatever shot fire at you, all that's left of it is ash."

"Is there anything in the lake?" I asked.

"We sent divers into the area where the explosion occurred, but they didn't find anything unusual," said Briar. "Maybe we'll send them back in tomorrow, but it doesn't seem promising."

"Has the ash been analyzed?" asked Duke.

"Lab's working on it." Briar turned and grabbed a slice of pizza after all. He must have been ravenous, because he bit off almost half the slice at once.

"Any hits on the missing persons network?" I asked.

Briar shook his head as he chewed and swallowed. "Nothing yet, but it takes time for a bulletin to circulate."

"So we've got nothing," I said, disappointed.

"Diddly doodly squat," added Duke.

Briar wolfed down another huge bite. "Meaning you're not having any luck either, I take it?"

"Not yet," I told him. "But Ashanti and I are going to see some friends of mine tomorrow. I'm hoping they can help."

"I wish *I* had friends like yours," said Briar. "While you're at it, ask if they could solve Ellie's murder, too, would you?"

"I'll see what I can do," I said.

"Keep me in the loop. I'll do the same." Briar finished off the crust of his slice and dusted off his hands. "Where are you two planning to stay tonight?" He nodded in Ashanti's direction.

"My place, probably," I said, though we hadn't discussed it.

"Wish I could offer you protection, but I can't spare anyone for the full detail," said Briar. "Best I can do is a periodic drive-by."

"We'll be fine," I said.

"With Earth Angel and Power Woman over there, I'd be more worried about anyone who's dumb enough to take them both on," said Duke.

Briar smiled. "I'm inclined to agree." He reached for my hand and gave it a squeeze. "But you call if you need me anyway." Leaning in, he snatched a kiss.

Then he spun, pulled on his hat, and headed for the door. "Good night, everyone." He opened the door to the sound of "Caravan" and gave us all a wave. "Let's get some rest and go at this fresh in the morning."

"Words of wisdom." Duke got up from his desk. "I suggest we all abide by them."

He was right and I knew it. If tomorrow was anything like today had been, I was going to need to be at the top of my game.

And yes, I was starting to feel tired. I was still rattled and wired about the attack at the lake and Ellie's murder by someone claiming to be me, but a deep weariness was settling into my core.

Time for rest, whether I liked it or not.

"Ashanti?" I said. "Are you okay with staying at my apartment? It's nothing special, but there's a guest room."

"Are you sure I won't be putting you out?" said Ashanti. "I could pull out a diamond and get a motel room or something."

"No worries," I told her. "Let's call it a wrap for tonight, everyone."

"I'll just stay and clean up," said Luna.

"You should get some rest," said Duke. "It's almost midnight."

"I don't mind if you don't." Luna grinned. "I'm a *total* night owl, you guys. I don't feel the *slightest* bit sleepy."

It was then Duke did something that surprised me.

"All right then, my dear Luna," he said. "We shall leave you to it."

I knew I was frowning, but I couldn't help it. Duke, who trusted no one but himself to watch over the office, was cavalierly turning it over to someone who was practically a stranger? It didn't add up.

"Remember to lock the door behind us when we leave," he told her. "And lock the place up tight when you go home."

"Don't worry about a thing," she said. "I've got it under control."

I stood there for just a moment, wondering if I should intervene. Did I trust Luna as much Duke did? Even if I did, was it smart to leave her there alone if someone was gunning for Ashanti and someone else had committed murder in my name?

Duke was the one who finally settled it for me. "Earth Angel." He winked and nodded for me to join him at the door. "Our new office manager can handle things just fine here."

"Office manager? I thought she was the receptionist."

"She's been promoted." Grinning, Duke nodded for me again. "No time like the present to start getting our money's worth out of her."

I sighed and headed for the door, waving for Ashanti to follow. Duke could get me to give in like nobody else. The friendship between us was the strongest I'd ever known.

As the three of us left, Luna shut and locked the door behind us. Smiling, she waved goodbye, then tugged down the blind behind the window. The blinds on the other windows along the front of the place were already down.

"Good night, Earth Angel," said Duke. "Good night, Ashanti."

"Good night, Duke," I said, and then I headed for the Highlander with Ashanti in tow, feeling a little like I'd just been turned out of my own place and no longer belonged there for reasons I couldn't fathom.

9

Ashanti and I hit the road around eight the next morning, heading west under bright blue skies. She'd slept soundly and seemed to be in good spirits, watching the passing scenery with the window down. She also looked a little fresher since I'd loaned her a change of clothes. The yellow dress, which had seen better days, had been swapped for a pink t-shirt and faded jeans. She was one size bigger than I, so they looked small on her, but the white sneakers we'd swapped her high heels with seemed to fit her just fine. Luckily, we wore the same shoe size.

Glancing over, I realized she looked just as regal in such casual clothes as she had in her dress and heels. She didn't have any makeup on, but her face was just as beautiful as it had been the day before with a full palette of cosmetics.

I sure didn't feel as regal as her in my own casual outfit—black t-shirt, black jeans, red sneakers, and brown leather jacket—though I figured I outranked her. After all, whoever she was at the core, I was still the human manifestation of the entire planet Earth.

"Have you heard from Sheriff Briar yet today?" she asked after a while.

"He texted me," I told her as I swung the Highlander in a hard left turn.

"Is there any news? About the cases?"

I shook my head. "He said he'll let us know if anything breaks."

Ashanti nodded. "Do you think he can solve these crimes?"

"He's a great cop," I said. "He helped me solve my best friend's murder and get out of a very bad situation." I left out the part about helping me save humanity from annihilation; it wasn't something I talked about with people I didn't know that well.

"Is that when the two of you got together? Became a couple, I mean?"

It surprised me a little that she'd asked, but I answered anyway. "Yes, as a matter of fact. That's when it happened."

"Good for you, Miss Glow." Ashanti smiled. "Good lovers are hard to find."

I felt myself blushing behind my sunglasses and changed the subject. "Why do you call me that? Why 'Miss Glow?'"

"Because of the glow, of course." She turned and scrolled her hand through the air alongside me. "Right there. So *bright*."

"Is that so?" I darted a glance her way from the corner of my eye.

"Oh *my*, yes." She poked a finger at the air a few inches from my shoulder. "All *around* you. Glowing and flowing all the time."

If she was telling the truth, it was news to me...though as the avatar of planet Earth, I couldn't rule it out. If it *was* there, why wasn't I aware of it, though?

"It's there right now?" I asked. "You can see it?"

"Don't worry." She reached over and lightly touched my upper arm. "It's a *good* glow, I'm sure of it. I've seen *bad* ones, and yours isn't like that at all."

"That's good to know, I guess."

"Why do you think I let you help me? Why do you think I trusted you? Why do you think I'm in the car with you now, though you haven't told me where you're taking me?" She gave my arm a squeeze. "Because even without my memory, I can recognize a good person with a good glow when I see one."

I felt a little awkward and kept my eyes on the road. Just in time, I spotted a sign for our destination, announcing it was just a mile up ahead on the left.

"That's where we're going," I said as we zipped past the billboard.

"'Doc Yowg's?'" It wasn't a shock she mispronounced it; most folks got it wrong the first time.

"It's 'Yock,'" I told her. "As in Doc Yough's Bar and Grill."

"What's to see at Yock's Bar and Grill?" She said it like it tasted funny.

"More than meets the eye," I said. "That's for sure."

A twenty-minute drive from Confluence, Doc Yough's Bar and Grill was smack in the heart of whitewater rafting country. Ohiopyle State Park, home of the Youghiogheny River with its famous rapids, was literally right across the road.

During peak rafting season in the summer, hordes of people roared into Ohiopyle and hit the wild Youghiogheny...but only a select few knew that Doc's was the *real* star attraction. Only those in the know had a clue that the *true* natural wonders lay inside that building with the log cabin front and the cedar shake sides.

As we rolled in off the road, I saw there were only three other vehicles in the gravel parking lot—a battered red pickup, an old Lincoln Town Car that was half burgundy, half gray primer, and a black BMW. The high-end coupe didn't surprise me at all; Ohiopyle was far enough south that it drew rafters, fishermen, and other outdoor lovers from as far as Washington, D.C. There were plenty of upscale lodgings and eateries to cater to them, too, though Doc's was more of a mid-range kind of joint.

As I led Ashanti inside, the place looked the way I remembered, which was much brighter than the average bar and grill. Pale wood, polished brass, gleaming mirrors, and white tablecloths filled the room, awash in light streaming in from expansive skylights and windows. It was like a dingy country bar had died and been reborn as a heavenly hangout for an angelic clientele.

As I'd expected from the looks of the parking lot, there were only a few customers on hand—a well-to-do middle-aged couple eating breakfast at a table on the far side of the room, a grizzled old man alone in a booth along the wall, and an old woman at the bar with a beer in front of her.

"Is one of them who we came here to see?" whispered Ashanti.

I shrugged and headed for the bar. "You never know in this place."

Just as I hopped onto a stool at the end of the bar, the door at the opposite end swung open, and a familiar face lunged out of the kitchen, a skinny young guy with two glass coffee pots in hand—one with a black spout, the other orange. His sunken-cheeked face was lost in a bushy forest of black hair and matching chest-length beard.

"Hey, Ashanti." I pointed at the man with the coffee pots. "Tell me, do you see a glow around *him*?"

She stared across the room, then smiled. "Not as bright as yours, but yes! Can you see it, too?"

"Just had a hunch," I told her.

As the bearded guy poured coffee for the couple at the table, he looked downright scrawny to me. Cords in his neck and forearms twisted and squirmed like snakes under the skin. His red plaid flannel shirt hung loose around his upper body, which was stuck in the waist of his jeans like a lollipop stick in a giant hoop skirt.

He noticed us in a general sense and rushed over without taking a closer look. He was in high gear, to say the least, not really paying attention to what to him were unnecessary details.

He was already looking over his shoulder when he spoke to us. "Coffee?"

"Thanks," I said. "I could *go* for a cup of mud."

"Regular or decaf?"

"Neither," I told him. "I want *actual* mud. A cup of *wet dirt* from the bed of the Youghiogheny."

Suddenly, he snapped to full alertness and really looked at me. "Gaia?" His eyes instantly lit with twinkles of sheer delight, and a bright-toothed smile parted his shaggy beard.

"Hi, Mahoney." Though he wasn't quite the man he used to be, I was still thrilled to see him, and then some. "I brought a friend."

Still smiling, he turned to Ashanti...and his mouth fell open in a look of pure shock. He dropped the decaf coffee pot from his left hand, but I jumped and caught it before it could hit the floor. The other pot shook, sloshing coffee all over as he stumbled back a step.

"Great Lady!" His voice trembled. "What are *you*...how could *you*...?"

Ashanti just sat there, confused and transfixed.

"I am so *honored*." Mahoney bowed his head. "You are *most* welcome here, Great Lady of the Canyon."

Ashanti shot me a look. "Is he talking to *me?*"

"I'll do everything I can to make you feel at home," said Mahoney, "though you are so very *far* from your own magnificent homelands."

"Mahoney?" I shoved the decaf coffee pot in front of his face to get his attention. "What the hell are you *talking* about?"

He looked at me like I was nuts. "But you're *with* her, and you're..." He lowered his voice. "You're *Mother Earth*. You *have* to know."

"Let's assume I don't."

"Really?" He looked like a wild-eyed prospector as he peered around the coffee pot at Ashanti. "You mean *you* haven't told her?"

"Told her what?" asked Ashanti.

"Okay." He took a deep breath then, and let it out slowly, regaining his composure. "All right." He nodded. "Excuse me if I overstep my bounds." He bowed his head to Ashanti, then turned to me. "Gaia...this woman is one of *my* kind. She is *Landkind*...and one of the greatest among us."

"I am?" said Ashanti.

He stared at her in disbelief, then shook it off. "She is the Great Lady of the Canyon," he said. "Though how she came to be *here*, I couldn't guess."

"Canyon?" said Ashanti.

"What canyon?" I asked.

This time, he didn't even try to hide being dumbfounded. "Which one do you think? The *Grand* one, of course!"

10

Doc Yough's was understaffed that morning, so we didn't get a chance to talk at length with Mahoney right away. While we waited, Ashanti and I sat at the bar drinking coffee and played a version of the game Twenty Questions, which was more like *Ten Thousand Questions*.

"What was Mahoney talking about, Miss Glow?" she asked. "What did he *mean*, I'm the Great Lady of the Canyon? What's Landkind? Why did he call *you...*"

"Whoa." I waved my hands to slow her down. "It's a long story. *I* don't even know what he means about the Grand..."

"How could I *be* the Grand Canyon?" she said. "It doesn't make any..."

"*Listen.*" I smacked the palm of my hand on the bar to cut her off. "There are special people in the world, okay? They contain the *essences* of *places*...the *souls* of mountains and rivers and valleys and islands...and *canyons*. They are a merging of *landforms* and *humankind,* otherwise known as *Landkind.*"

"Mountains in the form of people?" Ashanti scowled. "That doesn't even sound *real.*"

Leaning around, I gestured at Mahoney as he hurried into the kitchen. "Mahoney Wells is one of them. He encompasses the region known as Ohiopyle State Park. Youghiogheny River is his very heart and soul."

"But it's just dirt and water," said Ashanti. "Dirt and water can't *think* and *feel*."

"You'd be surprised," I told her. "Anyway, he wasn't *always* Landkind. When I first met him, he was just a human being who owned a travel agency. While helping me deal with some bad people at a place called Parapets—lunatics who wanted to wipe out mankind—he lost his humanity."

"And became Landkind?" asked Ashanti.

"More like a warped hybrid of man and rock." Remembering Mahoney in his Crossbreed form made me feel sick inside. The merging of human and mineral hadn't gone well in his case and had left him deformed and in perpetual agony. "I lost track of him in the chaos as we brought down Parapets. I gave him up for dead, in fact, but he turned up weeks later. Some friends of mine were able to undo *most* of the damage by giving Mahoney a fresh start as Landkind, replacing the original Ohiopyle avatar and owner of Doc Yough's, Owen Harkins."

She shook her head slowly. "And I'm like Mahoney? According to him, I'm Landkind, too."

"Apparently." I swigged the cold coffee in my cup.

"And I'm filled with the spirit of the Grand Canyon somehow."

"That's what Mahoney said."

For a long moment, she stared at the bar's polished surface. "Seems like something I ought to remember, doesn't it?"

"It does at that," I agreed.

"Then why don't I?" she asked.

It was a good question. "No idea."

Just then, Mahoney charged over and flung his arms open wide. "Finally caught up, ladies! We have a window of opportunity, so let's not let it go to waste."

"You're just in time," I said. "Ashanti needs someone to explain why she doesn't remember being the Grand Canyon."

"Good question." Mahoney walked behind the bar and stood facing us as he poured a glass of beer from a tap shaped like a boulder. "All I know for sure is, she's lucky her memory is *all* she lost."

"What are you talking about?" I said.

Mahoney filled the glass halfway and put it down for the head to settle. "There have been *disappearances*. Didn't you know, Gaia?"

I shook my head. "I guess I wasn't paying attention."

Mahoney nodded. "There've been quite a few who've gone missing over the past month or so. They just disappeared, leaving behind their geologic vessels—and those vessels are *emptied out*. It's like there's no *presence* bound to them anymore...no *mind* inhabiting the shell of the mountain or lake or what have you."

"I didn't know *any* of this," I told him. "Why didn't anyone reach out to me about it?"

"Landkind takes care of its own," he said. "At least we try to. But what's happening now..." He pushed his fingers through his bushy hair, leaned his bony elbows on the bar, and hung his head. "We need help, I don't mind telling you."

"I'm so sorry." I felt awful for not keeping better track of him after helping him heal and find a new life. I'd let so many people down, and they had ended up paying the price for my neglect.

"We've already lost Blue Knob Mountain, Deep Creek, and Rocky Gap," said Mahoney. "Their geologic vessels are empty, and their human forms are nowhere to be found."

"That's *terrible*."

"Why do you think I was so amazed when *she* walked in?" he said, looking up at Ashanti. "Not just because she's so far from home, but because she's the first Landkind to return after going missing. It's a *miracle* she's here at all."

"I don't understand," said Ashanti. "How do you know who I am if *I* don't even know?"

"Because we've met before today," explained Mahoney. "I visited the Grand Canyon once, and you rolled out the red carpet. It was a wonderful, wonderful visit."

Ashanti smiled. "I wish I remembered it, too."

I frowned as I tried to wrap my head around the facts we'd been given. "Mahoney, you said Ashanti was the first Landkind to return after disappearing. How did you know she'd gone missing in the first place?"

Mahoney sipped his beer. "There's a kind of *network* among the places of the Earth—channels through the rock and dirt and water, carrying messages in vibratory, chemical, and electrical form. When something happens that concerns us all, the alarm is sounded. Word is passed among us, and we *know*. In this case, we knew that the

Grand Canyon and others across the country had vanished without a trace."

"How many others?" I asked, playing with my braid.

"Dozens," said Mahoney. "And those are just the ones we *know* about."

I felt awful as the news sank in, as if the plight of the missing was my responsibility. I was Mother Earth, after all, and they'd disappeared on my watch. Could they have been saved if I'd paid closer attention to their lives?

Could they *still* be saved? "With so many missing from so many parts of the country, surely *someone* has tried to find them," I said.

"There've been a lot of search parties," said Mahoney. "In fact, a group from *this* area went out a few days ago. The same thing happened to all of them: gone without a trace."

"The local search party," I said. "Do you know anything about where they were going?"

"They were looking into a fracking site near Shawnee State Park," said Mahoney. "Run by a company called EarthSave Unlimited."

"EarthSave." The name made me sick. Was there any lie people wouldn't use to mask their environmentally destructive activities? "What did they say about this place?"

"Just that Deep Creek and Rocky Gap had talked about it before disappearing," said Mahoney. "Some kind of new *ultra-fracking* technique was secretly being used at the site, and they were worried about the damage it might cause."

Already, this was smelling distinctly clue-like. "Was the same ultra-fracking technique involved in any of the other disappearances?"

Mahoney frowned. "I don't know."

"Could you find out on the Landkind network?" I asked. "While Ashanti and I go do some research in Confluence?"

"I can try," said Mahoney.

"Good." I grabbed his beer and had a swig of it myself, then clomped the mug back down on the bar. "We're going to get to the bottom of this, Mahoney. We're going to find our people and bring them back."

"I hope you're right, Gaia." Mahoney smiled faintly but looked doubtful. "We've lost too many good ones already. I'd hate to think I'll never see *Phaola* again."

At the mention of the name, a wave of despair washed over me. Though I hadn't seen Phaola for some time, she was someone whose friendship I'd grown to treasure.

"Phaola led the local search party to the fracking site?" I said.

Mahoney nodded. "Laurel would have been proud."

"Phaola's the one who found me," Ashanti told him, "and sent me to Gaia. I was wandering in the woods with no memory, completely lost, and she found me and put me on the road to finding her."

"You don't remember anything before that?" asked Mahoney. "Anything about why you were out there in the woods to begin with?"

Ashanti shook her head. "Not really."

"Then I wonder how you got there," said Mahoney. "And how you're mixed up in all this."

"Mixed up?" said Ashanti.

"You *must* be," said Mahoney. "It isn't every day the Great Lady of the Grand Canyon wanders the Pennsylvania forest without any memory and gets directed to seek out the Earth Mother by the Lady of the Alleghenies."

11

I was tempted to go straight from Doc Yough's to the fracking site and let loose. After all, time might be running out for Phaola and the rest.

But I ended up driving back to Confluence with Ashanti instead. The Landkind who'd disappeared were not pushovers; Phaola, especially, was *extremely* powerful. Marching half-cocked into hostile turf that had claimed them might not be the smartest plan in the playbook.

But turning my back like that still sucked...especially because I'd been turning my back too much lately on good people who'd needed my help. A very wise woman had warned me about it time and again, telling me I needed to focus on watching over the world and Landkind because we were all in great danger.

That woman was Phaola, and I realized now that she'd been right. I'd been pretending my true nature didn't matter, that my personal life was more important than my friends and their well-being. Now look what had happened to them—to *her*.

I swore I'd come back and save them all before it was too late.

"Duke?" I called the office over the speakerphone in the Highlander as I pulled away from Doc Yough's. "I need you to get rolling on some research right away."

"Sure, Gaia." Luna, not Duke, had picked up the call. "What kind of research?"

I almost asked for Duke—then decided Luna must be trustworthy if he was letting her answer the phone. "Anything you can find on a fracking company called EarthSave Unlimited."

"EarthSave? Are you sure that's a *fracking* company?"

I smirked at Ashanti, who couldn't help listening in. "I'm sure," I said. "They're operating some kind of site near Shawnee State Park in Bedford County. Find everything you can on that, too."

"You got it, boss," said Luna. "When are you coming home?"

"We're on the way right now," I told her. "And we need to move on EarthSave ASAP."

"Roger that," she said briskly. "By the way, an F.B.I. agent was here to see you a few minutes ago. A guy named Frank Wagner."

I frowned. "What did he want?"

"He said something about recruiting you," said Luna. "And he mentioned meeting with you over lunch."

Frank had mentioned recruiting me at the site where I'd taken down Crystal, and now it sounded like he was serious. Either that, or he was coming on to me. Either way... "I don't have time for him right now. If he calls or drops by again, I'm not available."

"Understood," said Luna. "Anything else?"

"Negative," I told her. "Just get on that research and hold down the fort."

"Ten-four," she snapped. "Luna out!"

Just as she hung up, Briar dialed in, and I took the call. "Hey, Dale."

"Gaia." He sounded dead serious, positively grim. "I need to show you something. *Now.*"

Alarm bells were ringing in my head. "I'm on my way back from Doc Yough's. Still a couple minutes out from Confluence."

"Get here as fast as you can," he said. "And come alone."

The alarm bells were more like alarm *thunderbolts* now. "Where should I meet you?"

"At your place," he said. "It's about Ellie Grenoble."

I frowned, unable to guess what he wanted me to see—except that it had something to do with Ellie's murder. That fact alone made me drive faster.

"All right, Dale," I said. "I'll see you there."

"Come alone." He hammered the point home. "And hurry."

Without another word, he cut off the call.

"What was that all about, Miss Glow?" asked Ashanti.

"Beats me," I told her, putting even more pressure on the accelerator pedal. "But I guess I'll have to drop you at the office before I find out."

"I don't want to wait," said Ashanti. "Would it help if I commanded you as the Great Lady of the Canyon to take me along?"

"Briar still wins," I told her. "This is Pennsylvania, not Arizona. You are *way* outside your jurisdiction, Grand Canyon."

After depositing Ashanti at Cruel World Travel/Charmer Investigations, I raced straight to my place, parked behind Briar's cruiser, and hurried inside. The whole time I was in transit, my imagination ran wild, conjuring the possible things Briar might want to show me at the dead woman's house. None of them were good.

Briar had a key to my place, and he was waiting in the kitchen, looking about as grim as he'd sounded on the phone. "Hi, Gaia." He was leaning against the counter by the sink, sipping from a cup of coffee. Glancing at the coffeemaker, I could see he'd recently brewed a full pot.

"I came as soon as I could," I told him. "What did you want to show me?"

"These." He put down the coffee cup and stepped over to the kitchen table, where what looked like three fat scrapbooks were arranged in a stack. "They belonged to Ellie Grenoble. As soon as I realized what they were, I sneaked them out of the place."

Frowning, I approached the table. I could tell from the spines and edges that the books were in varying degrees of deterioration— the top one dark green and slightly worn, the one under it black and more ragged, and the gray one on the bottom frayed and ancient. I wondered what the hell lay inside them.

A feeling of dread washed over me as I sat at the table and stared at the books. "You removed evidence from a crime scene during a murder investigation?"

"It was important," said Briar. "You'll see."

I looked him in the eye and hesitated. Briar wasn't big on unnecessarily dramatic scenes. Whatever was in store for me, I had no doubt it was going to be a bombshell.

Reaching across the table, I slid the dark green book off the stack and put it in front of me with the spine facing left, cover side up. I took a deep breath and let it out slowly...again flicked my gaze from book to Briar to book.

And then I opened the cover.

And I was shocked to see myself staring back at me.

It was me in black and white, a clipping from a newspaper. I recognized it without checking the date on the clipping; it had been published five years ago, when I'd first come to town with Duke and opened Cruel World Travel/Charmer Investigations. In the photo, I stood in front of the storefront for those very businesses, grinning with pure joy on the cusp of a new beginning.

Travel Agent/Private Eye Sets Up Shop. That was the cutline under the photo. *Businesswoman Gaia Charmer offers travel planning and investigative services under one roof.*

I remembered it had been the first time I'd appeared in the local newspaper, *The Confluence Chronicle*. I'd been so happy and proud, so thrilled to launch what to me was the first adventure of my life. Because the truth was, in my current human incarnation, I hadn't been alive very long by then; though I'd looked to be in my early twenties, I'd only walked the surface of the Earth for a few weeks.

So I was practically a newborn in that photo pasted on page one of the book. It wasn't the first day of my life, but close to it.

Which, once the nature of the image fully registered, made me wonder. "What was *this* doing in Ellie Grenoble's house?"

"There's more," said Briar. "Keep going."

As I flipped through the pages, I saw one photo of me after another, one news story after another. In chronological order, they traced my life and career in Confluence, highlighting accomplishments (aiding in the apprehension of a killer), good deeds (sponsoring Earth Day events at local schools), and the occasional political action (talking to City Council about local water pollution). There was even a photo and story about my rescuing the kidnapped baby from Crystal Ruby Hayes.

What amazed me the most, though, were the stories about incidents I'd been involved with anonymously...the ones in which I'd used my powers to stop a crime or fend off a disaster or make a difference. I wasn't identified in these stories because I'd never taken credit or been seen in the process of working my magic. There was *no way* Ellie could have known I'd had anything to do with those events—yet there they were, pasted into the scrapbook right along with all the other moments from my life.

Stunned, I closed the scrapbook and looked at Briar. "What the hell?" I said.

"You understand now why I removed it from the crime scene?" Briar's face was stony, his eyes like steel. "A scrapbook about *you*, in the home of a woman who was *murdered* by someone claiming to be Mother Earth."

I shook my head slowly as the mystery took shape. "I barely *knew* this woman. How could she have been this *obsessed* with me all this time without me *knowing* it? And *why?*"

"All I know is, it's a good thing I found these first," said Briar. "They were hidden in a nook behind a wall panel, so the initial search missed them. I happened to notice a draft from around the panel and pried it open."

"I'd be a suspect," I said. "I *am* a suspect."

"We're in unknown territory here," said Briar. "I'd never expose you...but what if something else turns up?"

"Like what?"

He cleared his throat. "Something that implicates you."

Impossible, I wanted to say, but I hadn't expected the scrapbooks, either. Was this the true endgame of the crime—framing Mother Earth for Ellie's murder? If so, why? And who was behind it?

Uncertain of where events were taking me, I reached for the next scrapbook on the pile—the black one, which looked much older than the first. I slid it across the table, then hesitated to open the cover. The fact that Briar had brought it for me to see meant there had to be something important inside...perhaps something damaging.

But when I finally pulled the cover up and looked at the first page, I was more baffled than anything else. A newspaper photo was pasted there, but it was much older than any of the ones in the first scrapbook had been—and it wasn't a shot of me. Instead, the photo featured a slender woman with short, dark hair, performing on stage in a sequined black dress. Microphone in hand, she stood in the spotlight, belting out a song with such intense emotion that her eyes were pinched shut.

Below the photo, the cutline read: *Mid Silvergone Lights Up Cabaret!*

"Who's Mid Silvergone?" I flipped to the next page, and there she was again, as Auntie Mame. "I've never heard of her before."

"An actress and singer, apparently," said Briar. "She got her start in Pittsburgh in the mid-'70s."

I flipped another page and found a review of a 1977 production of *Fiddler on the Roof.* "What does she have to do with me? Why did you bring me this scrapbook?"

"The three scrapbooks were together in the nook," explained Briar. "I didn't recognize Mid Silvergone, but I figured I'd bring hers along because the other two are so interesting."

The other two? I closed the black scrapbook and reached for the gray one, the oldest of the three. This time, I recognized the woman in the yellowed newspaper photo on page one the second I saw it. She was much younger than the age at which I knew her best, but her face was unmistakable.

I didn't even need to read the cutline under the black-and-white photo to know who this appeared to be.

"Ellie Grenoble?" Her aquiline features were framed by blonde hair that was cut in a short, tight bob. She wore a gray sweater and a gray ankle-length dress, like something out of the 1930s or '40s.

Sure enough, the clipping was dated Wednesday, May 5, 1937. Doing the mental math, I quickly realized how impossible it was for Ellie to be in that photo.

"I'm guessing that's Ellie's mother," said Briar. "Though I haven't followed up on it yet."

The woman in the photo did look like she was at least in her mid-to-late twenties, though I couldn't be sure. She was standing in a classroom setting with a blackboard behind her and two children beside her—a little dark-haired boy and girl who looked like they were in second or third grade. The boy had a high-and-tight crew-cut, and the girl had baby doll curls on either side of her adorable face. Both kids were holding up an apple for her to take.

Apples for the teacher, read the cutline. *Miss Ellie Grenoble, English Teacher at Confluence Elementary, is rewarded for her efforts by prize students James Sydney and Hope Martin, both 8.*

"It couldn't be her." I kept staring at her face in the photo, mystified by the close resemblance.

"Wait till you see what else she did besides teaching," said Briar.

Turning more pages, I saw photos of Ellie in classroom settings and attending community events. Then, I came to a photo of her in a World War II military uniform, smiling.

Local Woman Serves as Army Nurse in Europe, read the cutline.

"She never told me her mother was in the war," said Briar. "She never mentioned her mother at all."

The pages after that were full of clippings from *Stars & Stripes,* detailing various battles and troop movements...plus commendations for Ellie. Eventually, the war-era stories ended, and I came to a new set of clippings—each one detailing an environmental incident or natural disaster of some kind.

They flew past as I flipped through the pages—flash floods, mudslides, forest fires, earthquakes, avalanches. One after another for dozens of pages, they paraded through history, always without any explanation as to why they were in the scrapbook at all.

"What the hell?" I said as the disasters kept coming. "Why would she even care about this stuff?"

"I don't know," said Briar, "but you should skip to the last page."

I did as he asked, exposing the last clipping on the final page of the gray scrapbook. And as I gazed at the photo and read the text, I couldn't help gasping.

"This is...I can't..." The headline read as follows: *Local Woman Missing.*

"See what I mean?" Briar said grimly.

I did...and I didn't. Because what I was seeing didn't make any sense.

Gaia Charmer Grenoble, 23, of Confluence, was reported missing on Friday. That was how the news story started.

And the photo that went with it...

"It's impossible," I told him.

"Is it?" he asked. "After all the things we've been through and everything you've told me about?"

I couldn't tear my eyes off that photo. The dateline above it read *June 6, 1947.* "Impossible." Even as I said the word, I couldn't deny what I saw.

I couldn't deny that the woman in the photo looked just like me…and I had no memory of living as a past incarnation with that name, appearance, and mysterious fate.

Hours later, asleep beside Briar as Ashanti slept in the guest room of my apartment, I dreamed about *her*. The woman who could have been my twin, whose photo I'd seen on the last page of the gray scrapbook.

I dreamed that I was in the office at Cruel World/Charmer Investigations, and she walked in the door, dressed in a World War II uniform. She wanted to arrange a trip to Germany, but not for her. She wanted *me* to travel there while *she* ran the businesses.

Then, suddenly, I was *in* Germany, wearing her uniform...but I liked it there. The people were drinking beer and dancing, and they all knew me. They'd known me my entire life, and they all *loved* me like family.

But then, somehow, I was lost in the Parapets compound, which was in the Bavarian Alps instead of Pennsylvania. And Phaola was supposed to meet me there, but instead she was screaming in the distance, her cries echoing over the snow-capped mountains. She was speaking Russian, for some reason, but I still understood what she was saying.

Save me, Ellie. Save me while you still can.

And then, breathing hard, I woke from the dream. Sunlight was glowing through the curtains, and Briar was gone.

And I had such chills racing through me that I pulled the covers over my head and shivered, fighting to get back to sleep.

The best thing about going into the office that morning was the coffee. A fresh pot of it sat in the coffeemaker, just when I needed it most.

Drawn by the aroma of blonde roast, I headed straight for the steaming pot like a shot. Without hesitation, I dumped coffee in my Earth cup, then added double cream and double sugar the way I liked. I didn't care who'd made it; I'd gotten up way too early and needed to caffeinate immediately.

"Good morning, everyone!" It was then I realized Luna was a big, fat liar. She'd said she was a night owl, yet there she was, bright-eyed and bushy-tailed first thing in the a.m. "Look what I have to go with the coffee!"

Lo and behold, she was walking out of the back room carrying a big, rectangular box from Hole in the Grounds, the awesome doughnut shop up the street. She put it on my desk and opened the lid, exposing all twelve perfectly hole-shaped goodies resting inside.

"Help yourselves," said Luna. "My treat."

I'd taken exactly one sip of Joe and still had my grouch on big time. "Where's Duke?" I knew I sounded grumpy and didn't care. "He should be here by now."

"I don't know." Luna shrugged. "I was here all night, and he never called in."

"You were here all night?" Ashanti sounded surprised.

Luna nodded. "Ever since Gaia picked you up and took you home with her."

"And I thought *I* didn't have a life," said Ashanti.

"You're sure Duke didn't leave a note?" Even as I asked, I checked the email on my phone for a message from Duke. The fact he wasn't there, and those close to me were in danger, had me worried.

"I'm sure." Luna left the room, then came back with paper plates. "He left no message, Gaia."

Duke had plenty of tricks up his sleeve and could take care of himself. That didn't make me worry any less...but I had to get moving with the business at hand. Other friends of mine were in greater danger still.

"All right then." I took a long swallow of coffee and let the warmth fill me like liquid sunshine. "Let me know when you hear from him, Luna."

"Ten-four, boss."

I reached for my favorite flavor of doughnut—chocolate honey-glazed—and took a bite. It was still warm, and I closed my eyes with pleasure as I chewed. "Let's talk about EarthSave Unlimited."

Luna cleared her throat and headed for her desk. "You were right about them, boss." She grabbed a tablet computer from the desk and flicked on the screen with the touch of her fingers. "They're all about the fracking."

"Tell me more." I sat down in my chair and savored another bite of delicious chocolate honey-glazed doughnut. It was just what I needed to take my Mother Earth mind off the scrapbooks Briar had brought to my apartment the night before.

"They started doing business two years ago." Luna read notes on her tablet. "They're based in Huntington, West Virginia, and have operations across the country."

"What about Shawnee State Park?" I asked.

"They currently have a site near there," said Luna. "There were pollution concerns, and a local environmental group briefly stalled the project, but then EarthSave pushed it through."

"What else?" I raised the doughnut for another bite. "Anything on this new ultra-fracking technique?"

"As a matter of fact, yes," said Luna. "Think fracking on steroids. Really *destructive* steroids."

"As if people needed to make fracking more destructive." I knew all about regular fracking, which used injections of liquid to break up solid rock and set free oil and natural gas. The drilling technique polluted groundwater, triggered earthquakes, and generally wrecked the Earth from the surface to the depths. I could only imagine what something called *ultra*-fracking might do.

"The big environmental groups are fighting it in court," explained Luna, "but they're not making much headway in the current climate of deregulation. If anything, the technique is spreading and becoming more popular than ever."

"So they'll just keep shattering more and more bedrock," I said with disgust. "They'll keep hollowing out the planet until it's just an empty shell, and then they'll wonder why it keeps swallowing them up."

Sometimes, I get so angry at the way humankind treats the world, I want to forget my own humanity and go on a damn rampage. It's about *time* I taught them a lesson, since they obviously won't listen to reason or common sense or compassion.

Could I do it? I've only tapped a tiny fraction of the power within the world, but I can *sense* the vast reserves at my disposal. If I were ever truly unleashed, it would be something to see. How could anyone even *fight* me? I'm the *planet* under their feet.

The better question is, *Could I go through with it?* And for now, at least, the answer is *absolutely not.*

For now.

"Luna, you said a local group was opposing the Shawnee area work." I polished off the last bite of my doughnut and emptied my coffee cup in one gulp. Luna's coffee, I had to admit, was every bit as good as Duke's. "Are they still active? Could you arrange for me to meet them?"

Luna flicked through content on her tablet and smiled. "Actually, it's just one woman." She held up the tablet, showing a photo of a heavyset young woman with bright green shoulder-length hair and dark-rimmed glasses with coffee saucer lenses. "Her name is Rune Ansel Carson, and she lives in the town of Bedford."

I liked Rune just from looking at her photo. Her eyes were bright and intelligent, and her lopsided grin made her look sarcastic. Plus, I guess it goes without saying that any friend of the Earth is quite literally a friend of mine.

"Make it happen." I got up from my chair and poured myself another round from the coffee pot. "Ashanti and I will head down to Bedford this morning to meet her."

"But I haven't spoken with her yet." Luna suddenly sounded flustered. "I don't even know if she's available today."

"She has to be." I grabbed another chocolate honey-glazed from the doughnut box. "The world needs her help."

Luna looked confused, then picked up the phone handset and made the call.

Just then, the door chime played "Caravan," and Agent Frank

Wagner stepped into the room. "Good morning, Gaia," he said cheerfully. "I'm glad I caught you in the office this time."

Instantly, my stomach knotted. I absolutely didn't have time for Frank, and I couldn't afford him sniffing around when sensitive business was in the works—sensitive *Mother Earth* business.

At least Luna had the common sense to hold off on her call to Rune Carson in Bedford. With a quick glance, I saw her hang up the phone and turn her attention to paperwork on her desk.

"Thanks for stopping by, Frank." I smiled, trying not to seem suspicious as I engineered an exit. "What can I do for you?"

He looked around and nodded. "Nice place you have here, Gaia." He chuckled. "And I love the fact it's part detective agency, part travel agency. You could hardly make it with just a *travel* agency in the age of online planning and reservations."

"We do all right." I sipped coffee and eased toward the front door. "So what's up?"

Frank stood between me and the door and planted his hands on his hips. "Recruiting, actually. I wanted to see if you might consider a career in federal law enforcement."

"I'm sorry, Frank." I winced a little. "I'm just on my way to a meeting."

"Well, is it something you think you might be interested in?" persisted Frank. "If so, we can set up a meeting of our own to explore the possibilities."

"Not really," I told him. "But thanks for thinking of me. I do appreciate it."

Frank stood there a moment longer, staring into my eyes. I felt like he was sizing me up, looking for more than my suitability as a potential agent for the Bureau. Maybe he *was* interested in me romantically, and the recruiting explanation was just an angle, a way in.

Whatever his motivation, he finally smiled and stepped away. "All right then." He gave a little bow and gestured at the door. "I don't want you to miss your meeting."

I was still getting a weird vibe from him, but I didn't have time to worry about it. As long as my friends were missing, I had to try to find them as soon as I possibly could.

"Thanks again, Frank," I told him as I backed toward the door. "Have a good one."

"You, too." Frank smiled and waved. "Stay out of trouble, Gaia Charmer. You know I'll have my eye on you."

"You probably will," said Luna. "I've *heard* about you government guys and your surveillance."

"We're a lot more out in the open these days." Frank chuckled. "Being sneaky just takes way too much effort."

1 3

An hour-and-a-half drive to Bedford later, I smiled when the doorbell of Rune's apartment played "What a Wonderful World" by Louis Armstrong. *Perfect.*

"Duke says that's my theme song," I told Ashanti, who just looked confused. "Though he also says that about 'Earth Angel' by the Penguins."

No one came to the door right away, and I looked around. The apartment was located in an old building on Main Street in Bedford, sandwiched between an upscale restaurant and a candle shop. Judging from the exterior, the place had seen better days—but at least it wasn't rundown or on the verge of being condemned.

Rune had said she'd see us at 10 a.m. Luna had texted me the time, and Ashanti and I were there right on the dot. Luna had been pretty persuasive on the phone, considering we were no doubt unknown quantities to Rune. For all she knew, we were anti-environmentalists hoping to start trouble.

"You really think she'll help us?" Ashanti straightened her outfit —the same faded blue jeans and white sneakers as yesterday with a pale green t-shirt instead of the pink.

"We're about to find out." I heard footfalls coming downstairs inside the place, and I cleared my throat to get ready.

A door chain slid out of its groove, a deadbolt clacked from its socket, and the door handle turned. The door swung open, and we were face-to-face with the green-haired, heavyset young woman from the photo. She wore black leggings and a baggy black t-shirt with an image of the Milky Way galaxy on the chest. An arrow pointed to a spot in one of the spiral arms, and the words "You Are Here" were printed across the midsection.

"Gaia Charmer, I presume?" Her voice was deep and a little raspy.

"You presume correctly." I extended a hand, and she shook it. "Great to meet you, Rune."

"The pleasure is all mine." Her lopsided smile looked just as winningly wiseass as it had online. "Love the name, by the way."

"Thank you." I grinned back at her, then turned to finish the introductions. "And this is Ashanti Moneta, my client. One of them, anyway."

"Hi, Ashanti." Rune let go of my hand and shook Ashanti's, then gestured behind her. "Won't you come in?"

"Thank you." I stepped into the little entryway with Ashanti and waited till Rune had done up the door chain and deadbolt again. The place had a musty smell to it already, I noticed.

One flight up, though, she led us through an unlocked white door, and everything changed. Her actual apartment was bright and airy and smelled like flowers. It wasn't a huge place, but it felt spacious from all the windows and mirrors on the walls. Best of all, there were plants everywhere, overflowing from pots and planters on every table, shelf, and counter.

Comfy. If I had to pick one word to describe her apartment, that's what it would be.

"Please, sit down." Rune gestured at an overstuffed brown sofa in the middle of the room. "Can I get you something to drink? An herbal tea, perhaps?"

"That would be fine," I said, and Ashanti nodded agreement.

Rune crossed the living room and stepped into the little kitchenette. "Luna said you wanted to talk about EarthSave?"

"We do," I told her. "Specifically, the drilling near Shawnee State Park."

"Where to begin?" said Rune. "It's a beautiful thing, if you like ruined watersheds, obliterated ecosystems, and the occasional earthquake in rural southwestern Pennsylvania."

"Other than all that," I said, "have you seen any suspicious activity?"

Rune filled cups from the spigot, put them in the microwave, and started heating them. "It doesn't matter. It's never enough to take them down, Gaia."

I shook my head. "That's not what I'm here for, Rune."

She folded her arms over her chest and frowned behind her huge dark-rimmed glasses. "Well, it damn well *should* be. If more people like *you* got involved—a respectable businesswoman and *celebrity...*"

I hesitated because she was right. When you got right down to it, what *was* I doing to save the environment? And I'm supposed to be *Mother Earth herself,* for cryin' out loud!

It wasn't like saving abducted children and stopping killers wasn't important, but my very *existence* was at stake.

Still, for now, I had to focus on the task at hand.

"Friends of mine are missing," I said. "They disappeared while investigating the Shawnee drill site. I want to find them before it's too late."

Rune was silent for a moment. The microwave dinged, and she took out the cups and dropped herbal tea bags in them to steep.

"It doesn't surprise me," she said finally. "Those so-called *Earth-Savers* are more like *scum* of the Earth."

"What kind of security do they have onsite?" I asked, fiddling with my braid. "Have you seen them apprehending anyone?"

"Some protesters, sure, but that was mostly in the early days. Are your missing friends protesters?"

"More like...reporters," I told her. "Investigating rumors of illegal activity."

"I like your friends already." Smiling, she took out the tea bags, put the cups on a red plastic tray with a sugar bowl and cream pitcher, and put it all down on a coffee table in front of us. "As far as security goes, they've got loads of it, and everyone's packing. I've actually heard of them chasing trespassers right into Shawnee State Park, searching campsites and picnics at gunpoint."

"That's pretty aggressive," I said, adding a spoonful of sugar and a splash of milk to one of the cups of tea. "But my friends aren't exactly pushovers." I gave Ashanti a meaningful look, knowing she'd understand.

"Well, there've been rumors." Rune sat in a yellow beanbag chair across from us. "Reports of some kind of *creatures* in the woods around the site. Maybe they have a basis in reality."

"You're saying these creatures might have attacked our missing people?" asked Ashanti.

Rune shrugged and spread her arms. "When you tamper with Mama Earth the way those *EarthSavers* do, I think scientific anomalies have got to be a possibility."

We sat in silence a moment, sipping our tea. "You've been inside, haven't you?" I asked, finally. "Could you help us get in there, too, past security, and find our friends?"

Rune narrowed her eyes and looked from one of us to the other. "I *might* be up for some trespassing...*if* I can trust you."

"I'm not trying to get you in trouble, if that's what you mean," I said.

"I've been a real pain in EarthSave's ass," said Rune. "I wouldn't put it past them to hire someone like you to set me up."

"If I *wanted* to hurt someone, it would be EarthSave," I told her. "I'll bet I'm more of an environmentalist than *you* are, even."

Rune locked her gaze with mine, measuring my reaction. "I had friends once, too, you know," she said grimly. "I lost them all because of EarthSave, one way or another."

"I'm sorry to hear that," I said.

"I'd like to help you find yours," said Rune. "But I swear to God, if you betray me, I'll make you *regret* it. Sooner or later, you'll *regret* it."

"That will never be a problem," I told her. "In the name of Mother Earth, I will *never* let you down."

A smile curled across Rune's face, and she nodded with satisfaction. "You just said the magic words, honey." She pushed up out of the beanbag chair and gave each of us a solid high five. "So when do you want to do this thing, anyway?"

"The sooner the better," I said. "You make the call."

"Then let's get on the road," said Rune. "Now's as good a time as any."

14

While Ashanti and I waited for Rune to get ready, I called Briar, but he didn't pick up. I settled for texting him about our plans, just in case things went sideways.

Though what I probably *should* have done was brought him into the mix before heading into danger. I probably should have brought in more help even than that...but I didn't. If we waited to pull together a team, the delay could be costly for Phaola and the others. Anyway, Ashanti and I were powerhouses, and I figured we could handle pretty much anything. Hopefully, Rune's guidance and information would help us make things work out right.

"Okay, kids!" Rune marched out of her bedroom in army-style olive-green camouflage togs and black work boots. "Who wants to go on a rescue mission?"

"Let's do it." Briefly, I wondered if I should let her know that Ashanti and I had abilities she might consider superhuman. Freaking her out in a life-or-death situation wouldn't be so awesome if it happened. On the other hand, trying to explain what we could do right now could get complicated and time-consuming. I decided to let it ride instead; maybe we wouldn't even need to use our powers, and the tricky questions would never come up.

Rune filled three water bottles (reusable aluminum ones, of course) and stuffed them in a tattered brown knapsack with a couple of energy bars. "Just remember, if any security goons approach us, we're birdwatchers, and we think we're still in Shawnee State Park. Even if we're on the EarthSave side of the line, stick to the story and we'll be fine."

"Sounds like a plan," I said.

"Glad we're on the same page." The lopsided smile returned to Rune's face as she fist-bumped me and Ashanti. "Let's light this candle, amigas."

Rune did most of the talking as we rode out to Shawnee State Park in my Highlander. She told us more about her commitment to the environment and her battles with EarthSave; she talked about growing up in the area and wanting to preserve its natural beauty at any cost. She said it was everyone's duty to fight back in every way they could to keep the environment alive and thriving.

I wondered what she'd say if she knew she was making Mother Earth feel disappointed in herself. Because that's how I felt when I listened to her. I'd been so wrapped up in the worries and routines of my human side for so long, even after discovering my true heritage, that I hadn't thought much about fighting back against those who would harm me. I might have stopped Groundswell and Atlantis from remaking the world in their own dark image six months ago, but I hadn't used my newfound power and stature to the utmost to continue the fight.

Though maybe I still didn't fully understand my true nature. Again, I thought of the photo at the end of the gray scrapbook, the image of a woman in 1947 who could have been my identical twin. What if a deep connection existed between us? What if there was more to my life than I'd imagined? What if my actual mission in the world was much different than I'd thought?

That would explain a lot, wouldn't it? But it wouldn't make me want to rescue Phaola and the other missing Landkind any less.

There were some things that would *never* change about me.

Rune knew the park like the back of her hand and pointed the way without hesitation. She guided us past the lake with its beach and docks—all still closed for the season—and took us deep into the heavy forest, aiming for the far rear corner of the park.

The paved road turned to dirt, and the dirt road became a rutted trail used by quads and dirt bikes sneaking into the park. After a while, we just pulled between some trees and parked the Highlander. If there was anything to mark the spot as a parking place, I didn't see it. As far as I could tell, Rune just *knew* where to go.

It felt good, then, to get out and stretch among the trees and forest creatures. "Reception" was good, as I liked to say, meaning I could sense the ebb and flow of the world around me much better than I could in a town or city.

At least I could until the ground shook under my feet.

"Welcome to the Shawnee Andreas fault!" said Rune as she grabbed hold of a fat tree trunk. "A Pennsylvania state park with no history of seismic activity."

The tremor started as a modest rumble and quickly intensified. I swayed as I worked to keep my balance. "All thanks to ultra-fracking, huh?"

"Ultra-fracking," said Rune, deepening her voice like a radio announcer reading a commercial. "When you want *your* quakes to come on *stronger* and last much *longer* than with plain old everyday *fracking!*"

Ashanti held on to the side of the Highlander, even as it bumped back and forth on its suspension. "But I don't hear any drilling noise," she said. "Shouldn't there be more noise?"

"Ultra-fracking is ultra-quiet," said Rune. "It's one of the selling points. It's how EarthSave was able to convince the state to let them frack so close to a state park. Never mind the *earthquakes*, right?"

The rumbling got even stronger, and I decided I'd had enough. Focusing my senses and mind, I reached down into the ground, following the vibrations below the surface. They led me on a jagged path, following the fractures in the rock—gliding toward the point of greatest pressure and friction.

I saw it up ahead like a wound in the crust of the world...a needle pumping a mix of water and grit into the deep, deep channel. Solid rock split and liquefied under that intense bombardment, releasing bursts of oil and natural gas to surge up and fill the crevices left by the blasts.

With my mind's eye, I sighted on that web of fissures and breaks, building up my own inner force like a seething fireball. Just when I felt I could no longer contain it, I unleashed the power dead-on at the gaping red wound, expecting to smash the injector and stop the quake.

Instead, the fireball went halfway to the target and fizzled, losing most of its power. It sputtered the rest of the way, shedding even more energy...and by the time it reached the drill site, its charge was gone.

And I had a splitting headache.

"What the *hell?*" What had just happened should *not* have happened. Was the site protected somehow? Were other forces at work in this situation?

In spite of all my power, I'd accomplished nothing. The quake rumbled on for another few minutes, then finally faded out on its own.

"Will there be aftershocks?" asked Ashanti as she pushed away from the Highlander.

"There usually are, but they tend not to be so bumpy." Rune let go of the tree and dusted off her camouflage. "No reason not to get on with our birdwatching, ladies. What do you say?"

I hesitated, wondering if there *was* a reason to turn back. My power had been drained in a way I'd never seen before. Was Earth-Save a greater threat than I'd guessed?

Phaola was no pushover. No Landkinder was, for that matter. Whatever had made them disappear must have been formidable.

For the first time, I found myself wondering if it was too formidable for Ashanti and I to handle.

"Gaia?" Rune pulled a bottle of water from her knapsack and flicked the pour spout open. "Are you ready to go scope out those triple-breasted blue butthatches we've come to watch?"

Staring in the direction of the drill site, I shot my mind down into the ground, feeling for a clue to whatever had stalled my attack. I sensed the same network of jagged fissures under the surface, the same welt of shattered rock bubbling with oil and natural gas. Everything was just like before.

Only *something* had sapped my power. *Something* had shrugged off Mother Earth as if she were no more threatening than a feather.

But my friends were out there somewhere, and I couldn't give up on them. This might be my last chance to bring them back alive.

Withdrawing from the underground channels, I winced at my headache and turned to Ashanti. "How are you feeling?" I asked.

"Better now that the earthquake's over," said Ashanti.

"All right then." I nodded at Rune. "Let's go get those birds."

Rune swigged some water, then closed the spout and tucked the bottle in her knapsack. "Stick with me, tweetheads." She whistled a rough birdsong, raising and dropping the pitch several times. "We'll find those mother-pluckers if it's the last thing we do."

15

The further we walked through the woods, the worse my headache got. It took up residence in the middle front area of my head, in the vicinity of my sinuses, and just wouldn't let up.

If Ashanti and Rune were experiencing anything similar, they didn't mention it, and I didn't ask. Heading into a dangerous situation, the last thing I wanted to do was give my teammates cause for concern.

Pushing the pain down as best I could, I kept going, hoping I'd be at full strength when push came to shove.

"Are we out of the park yet?" Ashanti asked after a while.

"We've been in enemy territory for a long time now," said Rune. "Didn't you notice the dark shadows hanging over everything, sucking the life out of your soul?"

"Oh, right," said Ashanti. "I thought those were just mosquitos."

I didn't laugh, because there was some truth to Rune's words. The closer we got to EarthSave's facility, the more its dark influence overshadowed me. The headache got worse, and so did the sense of foreboding.

"Hold up," I said eventually, when I sensed we were almost out of the woods. "You've taken us far enough, Rune. Let's split up here, and you can meet us back at the car when we're done."

"Nope." Rune grinned and adjusted her big glasses. "You don't think I'm gonna just *ditch* you guys, do you?"

Scowling, I rubbed my temples, but the headache wasn't going anywhere. "I don't want you getting hurt. This isn't your fight."

"It is if I *say* it is," said Rune. "Now shut up and get going, *both* of you."

"Rune, please," I said. "Just describe the facility in detail so we know what to expect, then hold down the fort until we get back. And if we *don't* get back, call in the cavalry. Call Sheriff Briar in Confluence."

"Bite me," said Rune, and then she pushed past us, continuing on course toward the EarthSave facility. "There's no way you're leaving me behind."

Ashanti watched her go and shrugged. "I guess she told *us.*"

For a second, I thought about trapping Rune in a sinkhole until we got back—but I changed my mind. I wanted to keep her out of the line of fire, but I also didn't want to hurt her myself in the process.

Not to mention, I respected that kind of pig-headedness. It reminded me of myself.

"Let's go." I nodded in Rune's direction and fell in behind her. "We've got people to rescue."

We walked a little further, and the woods melted away, leaving us exposed at the edge of a vast open space. A wide, weedy field stretched out before us, with a tall metal spire jutting from the middle of it. It was the exact injector/drill structure I'd seen and attacked earlier, source of my headache and faltering powers. Physically closer to it than ever, I winced as my headache amplified to its highest level yet.

Various trailers and buildings were arranged around the central tower. Rune pointed to the closest one, a long shed with corrugated gray plastic walls. "That's where we're heading first," she said. "There's a blind spot on this side, no cameras. As long as we stay in this wedge, we can sneak right up and scoot in the side door." She held out her hands in a "V," the open mouth of the shape facing the shed.

"Is that where they keep prisoners?" asked Ashanti.

"Last time I was here, it was part canteen, part infirmary," said Rune. "But we gotta start somewhere."

Reaching out with my senses, I strained for a mental snapshot of what was inside that shed. I should have gotten one in a heartbeat, reading the displacement of dirt underneath the structure and the vibration of rock and water to determine the number of people and inanimate objects within those walls.

But for once, I got next to nothing...just a muddy blur of objects and bodies. It was like someone had stuck a helmet on my head to interfere with the signals I was trying to tap.

"Ready?" asked Rune, and we nodded. "Then let's go. I don't see any security staff nearby, so let's run before the window of opportunity slams shut."

As we charged across the field, the ground rumbled again, jarring my strides. Looking up, I saw the injector/drill apparatus was in action, whirling and driving into the ground. Up close, I could hear it wasn't completely silent, that it made screeching and crunching noises while it worked—but it was still amazingly quiet for such a massive, destructive machine.

The three of us made it to the gray shed without a problem and paused there as the rumbling grew stronger. Then, Rune waved, and we followed her around the corner and through a side door there.

Once inside, we saw we were indeed in a makeshift, deserted canteen. There were four round, gray tables, each big enough to seat six or seven people, and a couple dozen gray plastic chairs. A refrigerator hummed in the room's far corner, alongside a counter occupied by a microwave oven and coffee maker.

Rune crossed the canteen for a look out a window facing the drill site. Then, she proceeded to the door in the far wall, leading deeper into the shed.

She opened it slowly, peered through the crack, then pushed it open the rest of the way and walked through. Following her across the still-rumbling floor, I saw the next room was an infirmary as she'd remembered, complete with exam tables, medical monitors, instruments, and first aid supplies.

"Where to next?" I asked, keeping my voice low. "Is there some kind of security trailer where they might hold suspects?"

Rune nodded. "There's a security shed over that way." She pointed in the direction away from where we'd entered. "I've seen them haul trespassers in there before."

"Sounds like a good bet then." I crossed the infirmary to a door that had a small window at eye level and led outside. "Though who knows if they're even here at this site at all, the way..."

Suddenly, the side of the shed wrenched violently outward. It broke away from the roof and peeled down, the corrugated plastic splitting as it plunged toward the ground.

At which point I realized the search was over. We had found the missing friends we'd come to rescue, alive and well.

Or, rather, they had found us. And they didn't look friendly at all.

16

Phaola hovered in midair, looking mightier and more beautiful than ever. Her slender form, clad in some kind of silvery, clinging spandex, was surrounded by a shimmering aura. Her long blonde hair with its icy blue highlights flowed and crackled with power, writhing around her head like a fiery halo. Her eyes pulsed with a silver glow that made them seem closed-off and challenging, not at all friendly or welcoming.

On her right stood a heavyset man with jet black hair, wearing black spandex. I recognized him instantly as the avatar of Prince Gallitzin State Park—a Landkinder who no longer looked as kind and gentle as I'd known him to be. Back hunched, head bowed, he clenched his fists and pawed at the ground like a bull getting ready to charge.

At Phaola's left, a middle-aged man with sandy hair and a trim beard stood tall in brown spandex, his hands and forearms enveloped in sparking golden light. I knew him as Blue Knob Mountain, another local avatar and man of great kindness—though the look on his face spoke only of hatred and rage.

None of them looked happy to see us. None of them looked like they were glad to be rescued.

Though I knew we couldn't take that for granted. "Phaola?" I said. "It's me, Gaia. We've been looking all over for you."

Phaola bobbed on currents of air and power, considering my

words. She frowned for a moment, and I thought maybe I'd gotten through to her, that the challenge in her fiery eyes had just been due to momentary confusion.

Then, the frown disappeared, replaced by a blank and icy abyss in the shape of her face.

Where this was headed, I no longer had any doubt.

"Are you sure *these* are your *friends?*" asked Rune.

"Something's happened to them," I told her.

"My memory was somehow erased when I went missing," said Ashanti. "I wonder if the same thing happened to them."

"By the way," said Rune. "You never *told* me your friends had *superpowers.*"

It wasn't the time or place to have a conversation about the nature of Landkind. "Get out of here!" That was the only thing Rune needed to know right now, before the shit hit the you-know-what. "Right now!"

"Like hell!" snapped Rune. "I'm in this whether you like it or—"

Before she could finish her sentence, Phaola flung up her arms, and deafening thunder boomed around us. She wove her fingers in a complex pattern, sending up sparks, and lightning flared across the sky.

Then came the rain. As a Hyade nymph, she controlled water and related weather in all its forms; that power had been multiplied a thousandfold since her ascension as the Lady of the Alleghenies.

A downpour of blistering intensity crashed upon us, instantly soaking us to the skin. It came down so hard, it *hurt;* it felt like thousands of tiny teeth chipping into my flesh in a relentless bombardment from above.

"Take cover, Rune!" I shouted through the roar of the murderous shower. Even as the words left my lips, I was reaching into the ground with my mind, grabbing the shelf of rock below the topsoil and fighting to tear it asunder.

But then my concentration was shattered as Prince Gallitzin State Park rammed into me with terrible force.

His weight flung me into the mud and planted me there. Before I could pull up rocks and bash him away, he jammed one utility pole of an arm into my throat, cutting off my air.

Thrashing in his grip, I struggled to break him away, still half in shock at the fact that my good friend was trying to kill me.

Dark spots danced in my eyes. I reached with my power into the earth, trying to make it lurch up under us and pitch him away...but it kept slipping from my grasp. What was *wrong* with me?

Then, before he could kill me, a beam of golden energy blasted into him, knocking him away like a speck of dust.

Gasping for breath, I turned and saw Ashanti hovering nearby. She was the one who'd saved me—but she faced another problem now. Blue Knob Mountain unleashed rays of searing energy from his own fingertips, catching her dead in the chest. Crying out, she spun away from the blast, leaving a trail of smoke curling behind her.

"Gaia!" Rune ran over and helped me to my feet. "Are you all right?"

I shooed her away, my gaze flashing to Phaola. My view of her was blurred by the curtains of heavy rain.

"I said to run!" I told Rune. "I can't protect you!"

"I'm an eco-warrior!" Rune shouted. "Chickenshit isn't in my vocabulary!"

The ground shook from the still-churning ultra-fracking tower, and lightning blazed. Phaola clapped her hands, and thunder rolled and crashed louder than ever.

Twirling her hands overhead, she created a pair of waterspouts, then slashed her arms down and sent the spouts shooting toward me. Digging deep, I managed to dredge up a sheet of mud-encrusted bedrock as a shield—but I got it only half as high as I wanted. I had to duck down behind it to avoid the worst of the spouts' propulsive force; even then, I was buffeted by their punishing wakes, pummeled behind the bedrock.

"Surrender!" shouted Phaola—or whoever was in control of her. "Surrender or be destroyed!"

As she fanned her hands wide with palms facing me, the rain turned to golf-ball-sized hail, coming down just as fast but with more painful physical impact. Wobbling as the ground underfoot continued to shake, I tried turning the bedrock I'd raised into a protective suit of stone—to no avail. I pulled some of the rock around me, but I couldn't flex it into the right shape to contain my body. Hunks of it kept falling away until I gave up trying to mold it.

At that moment, Prince Gallitzin State Park charged out of the dense hailstorm and plowed into me, flinging me over the mucky ground. I hurtled into the metal side of a construction trailer, leaving a dent as I bounced off and splattered into the slop.

I pried myself out of the mud just in time to see Prince Gallitzin State Park racing toward me again with fists extended. Head pounding like mad from the beating I'd been taking and my proximity to the ultra-fracking spike, I had trouble summoning the focus to pour my earth-based powers into stopping him.

But all I really needed was the tweak I managed to transmit. Reaching out, I drew up oil from underground into the mud in Prince's path, making it much more slippery. His black-booted feet skimmed over the oily slick and lost all traction, sliding out from under him. Shouting in surprise, he flipped over backward and went down hard, slamming into the muddy ground like a bull dropped from a helicopter.

Squinting through the hail, I saw his eyes were shut, and I felt relieved—as relieved as I could while being peppered with hail and threatened by a powerful ex-friend even as my own powers were on the fritz.

That slight relief lasted all of thirty seconds. Suddenly, the soggy muck flash-froze under me, locking me in place on my knees. The golf-ball-sized hail changed to *baseball-sized*, absolutely *pummeling* me as I fought to bat it away with my arms.

I took monster hits to my head, back, and abdomen. Mentally scrambled, I couldn't haul up a rock shield to deflect or capture them, couldn't stop the bludgeoning assault.

The next thing I knew, Phaola was hovering right above me, bathed in light. "Prepare to die." Even as she said it, her features looked eerily serene, utterly unlike any expression I'd ever seen on her face before.

Peering through the hailstorm, I saw Ashanti battling with Blue Knob Mountain, lashing out at him with energy bolts that he repelled with bolts of his own. They were locked in a stalemate; she wouldn't be helping me anytime soon.

I reached down again into the earth, grasping for anything that might help me. Every time I got a grip on something with my powers, the earthquake or hailstones or lightning smashed my focus to bits, and I lost it.

I started to realize this could be the end of the road for me. It was possible Phaola might kill me at any moment. Mother Earth would surely cast another avatar, but my particular human form would be eliminated.

I made one last try to save myself, barely stirring a nearby pile of gravel. Then, as Phaola raised her arms, and a blazing charge of power flared around her hands, I gulped in a deep, deep breath and held it, awaiting my end.

The charge burned brighter. Phaola clenched her teeth. I saw the muscles flex in her arms as she got ready to fire.

Then, without warning, *something* swooped out of nowhere and collided with her, blowing into her upper body.

Howling, Phaola dropped, plunging into the mud below. The spherical object that had bowled her over looped around and hurtled down for another strike, clipping her so hard in the head that she flopped unconscious into the mud. The hailstones stopped falling immediately, and the thunder and lightning ceased.

Only then did the object unfurl, revealing it had been a *person* all along—someone curled up into a ball. A *woman.*

It wasn't Ashanti, and it wasn't Rune, either. It was someone completely unexpected, someone who shouldn't have been anywhere *near* the EarthSave site.

"Gaia!" She zipped down to my side with a look of deep concern on her face. "Are you all right?"

I frowned up at her as she reached out a hand to help me. "I am, thanks," I told her. "But what the *hell* are *you* doing here, *Luna*?"

1 7

A *boom* like a bomb going off echoed through the drill site, tearing my attention off Luna. Looking toward it, I saw Blue Knob Mountain rocketing over the field, propelled by an awesome blast from Ashanti, and crashing into the injector/drill apparatus. The impact was so great, the spire buckled and snapped, toppling in pieces into the muck at its base. As it came down, a jet of black oil sprang up from the hole it had straddled, pouring up into the sky.

Finally, all three of our opponents were down—but it brought me no joy. Possessed or brainwashed, they were still my good friends, and I hated that we'd hurt them. Also, I realized that taking them down was just the start of our worries.

"Sorry, Gaia." Luna helped me to my feet and compulsively brushed mud off my leather jacket. "I had a feeling you were going to need help, and I couldn't just stay behind at the office while you—"

"*Stop.*" I had some big questions for her, but now was *not* the time. Our little expedition had gone about as far sideways as it possibly could, and the clock was ticking on how much worse it was going to get. "We don't have time for this."

Pushing her away, I fought through my pounding headache—so much worse since the fight—and tried to think. We could not have landed in a bigger mess if we'd tried.

"Rune!" I looked around and spotted her standing by a shed, staring. "I need your help!"

Rune's eyes narrowed. "Who the hell *are* you people, anyway? What's with all the flying and shooting energy beams and—"

"*Cameras,*" I snapped. "Where are the *security cameras?*"

Rune shrugged. "Every shed and trailer has one. They're networked wirelessly and upload their feeds to a cloud server via web app."

I slumped. "So the video of all this has already gone out. No way to erase it."

"Correct," said Rune. "There's no onsite server we can scrub, if that's what you're getting at. The web app's hackable, though, so maybe later we can—"

"Okay. Next order of business. We need to get out of here, and we need to take *them* with us." I pointed in the direction of Phaola, then Blue Knob and Prince Gallitzin State Park. "And we need to keep them *unconscious.*" Having them wake up in their current states without restraint could be a true disaster.

"Gaia?" Luna tapped me on the shoulder.

I brushed her aside. "We need a tranquilizer or something, but—"

This time, Luna was the one cutting *me* off. "Gaia!" Instead of tapping, she shook my shoulder roughly.

"*What?*" I swung around to face her, annoyed.

"I can *help!*" said Luna. "I'll take *care* of it."

"What are you talking about?" I said.

Before I could duck out of the way, she shot out a hand and touched the palm of it to my forehead. Suddenly, everything went black.

The next thing I knew, my eyes were fluttering open, and the blackness was gone. I felt someone holding on to me, keeping me from dropping in the slop underfoot.

And that someone was Luna.

"See what I mean?" She smiled. "I can keep them under or knock them back out with a touch."

I stood up and straightened my clothes, then jogged through the mud to where Phaola had fallen. Why she could do what she did, I didn't know, but I couldn't worry about it just then. All that mattered was, she was the solution to our problem.

"Ashanti!" I shouted to the woman hovering nearby. "Can you carry one of them?"

"Absolutely, Miss Glow." Ashanti drifted over to the inert form of Prince Gallitzin State Park. She extended both hands, suffused with golden glow, and slowly raised them. A flickering radiance surrounded Prince Gallitzin State Park, and he floated up from the mud, arms hanging limp at his sides.

"Rune and Luna, carry the other one!" I yelled over my shoulder. "If you can."

Crouching beside Phaola then, I put my arms around her shoulders and the backs of her knees. Grunting, I scooped her out of the mud and straightened, adjusting my grip.

Turning, I saw Luna hefting Blue Knob Mountain and slinging him over her shoulder like he weighed nothing at all. Rune tried to help, but Luna just waved her off with a smile.

As dire as our situation was, I couldn't wait to get to the truth about that platinum-haired mystery woman.

"Let's go!" I shouted, trudging through the slop toward the tree-line from which we'd first emerged. "We need to get back to the car and get rolling ASAP."

"What about the Sheriff?" asked Luna, who'd quickly caught up to me in spite of the weight on her shoulder. "Couldn't he just take care of all this?"

I stopped and looked back at the wreckage of the drill site. "I'm not sure I'd bet the farm on that," I told her. "We just demolished a ton of private property."

"Fighting super-powered, brainwashed kidnap victims," said Luna.

"I'm not hanging around to find out how *that* plays, and I suggest *you* don't, either." Phaola's body was heavy, and I followed Luna's example by shifting it to my shoulder. Normally, it wouldn't have been a problem to raise up a layer of rock or stones from the ground and use that to levitate the burden with my Mother Earth powers. This time, though, as hard as I tried, the substance of the world refused to cooperate. Lugging Phaola by hand was the best I could manage.

"But if cameras caught everything, EarthSave already knows it was us," said Luna. "They can already track us down based on the video."

"Let's not make it easy for them," I said, and then I resumed course for the woods. The border of Shawnee State Park wasn't far once we crossed the treeline. Then it was a matter of getting to the Highlander and making like a bat out of hell.

18

I was as surprised as anyone when we rolled into the alley behind Cruel World Travel/Charmer Investigations, all in one piece. Even burdened by the dead weight of unconscious friends, we'd made it to the Highlander, driven out of Shawnee State Park, dropped off Rune at her apartment (promising to get back to her later), and gotten back to Confluence without any mishaps.

Hopping out, I made sure the alley was empty, then unlocked the building's back door. Luna and Ashanti helped me quickly unload the three bodies and haul them into the back room, where we laid them on the floor. Then, alone, I hurried back out to move the Highlander to its parking spot on Casselman Street in front of the place.

Only then, with the Highlander parked and the engine off, did I allow myself to relax the slightest bit. Slumping forward, I rested my forehead against the wheel and took deep breaths, fighting to calm myself.

Even though I knew my freedom could still end at any moment. Security cameras at EarthSave's drill site had captured my performance and beamed it to the cloud. How long would it be until EarthSave identified me and tracked me down?

And how much good would I be when they got here if my powers didn't return in full? Even here, far from the ultra-fracking apparatus, I was still out of touch with the source of my strength, the Earth itself.

Would Phaola say it served me right? After all, I'd been slacking off in my role as Mother Earth for a long time. I'd already been out of touch with the Earth before losing my connection in the fight. Phaola had been the one who'd chided me about it again and again, but I'd been too busy with my life as a private eye and travel agent to pay much attention.

Now *she* had paid the price. I should've been watching more closely, guarding over my charges, and I'd *failed* them instead.

Pull yourself together, Gaia.

Leaning back, I took one more deep breath, let it out slowly, and got out of the Highlander. The day wasn't going to get any less difficult if I put off what I had to do next.

I unlocked the front door of the offices, stepped inside, and locked it again behind me. The window blinds were down, and I left the lights off to discourage passersby from taking interest. It was 7:30 in the evening, well after closing time, but folks had a way of stopping by if they thought we were still open.

When I entered the back room, I found Ashanti and Luna standing over the three bodies on the floor, looking grim.

"You can definitely keep them asleep?" I asked Luna. "Without hurting them?"

She nodded. "You bet your ass, boss."

"I wish we had some cots in this place," I said. "Or some blankets and pillows, at least."

"Can't help you there." Luna gestured at the bodies. "If I don't stay close, they might wake up."

"I'll run and get them," I told her. "Plus whatever else we need."

"Clean clothes would help." Ashanti was right. Phaola, Prince Gallitzin, and Blue Knob were muddy and bloody from the fight at the drill site, and so were we. Then there was the upholstery in my Highlander, which I tried not to think about.

"Other than that, what's next?" Luna looked expectantly at me. "Now that we have your friends back, what do we do with them?"

I leaned against the wall and folded my arms across my chest. "I don't know. I don't even know what's been done to them."

"Was the same thing done to me?" Ashanti gazed down at Phaola, her expression grave. "That's what I keep asking myself."

"You didn't turn into a killing machine," I said.

"Maybe I was *supposed* to," said Ashanti. "Maybe it didn't take, or they didn't finish the process."

"We need to get to the truth, whatever it is," I told her. "For your sake as well as theirs."

"But how do we do that?" asked Ashanti.

I thought for a long moment, considering the situation. Thankfully, my headache was finally letting up, so at least I could think clearly.

"We bring in a specialist," I said. "If we can find one in time, that is."

"What kind of specialist?" asked Ashanti.

"The *good* kind," I said. "One who can help you with *your* issue, too, hopefully."

Ashanti got a funny look on her face, as if she wasn't sure that would be a good thing or not.

With that, I pushed away from the wall and headed through the doorway to the front office, gesturing for Luna to follow. She joined me at the coffee maker on the counter, where I went to work starting a fresh pot of java.

"So tell me," I said, keeping my voice low as I poured coffee grounds into a white paper filter. "What's your story, office manager?"

Luna already had a pot full of water set aside from before and poured it into the top of the coffeemaker. "Isn't it enough that I'm here to help you?"

"Not a chance." I slid out the plastic filter basket and stuck the filter in it. "Who are you really? What's with the powers?"

Luna sighed and leaned against the counter. "I didn't plan to have this discussion yet," she said. "I'm not ready. It's not *time*."

I shot her a glare. "Do I look like I give a shit?" I slid the filter basket into its slot in the coffeemaker with extreme prejudice, and Luna jumped. "You need to *tell* me. I've got *enough* unknowns to deal with as it *is*."

Luna met my gaze nervously. "I'm not an unknown to you," she said. "In your heart, I think you already know who I am."

"I don't." I shook my head. "The first time I met you was three days ago."

"You really believe that, don't you?" She looked sad. "Your memory's no better than Ashanti's, is it?"

I flipped the switch on the coffeemaker, and it started percolating. "Just tell me," I said firmly. "Who are you and what do you want?"

Luna smiled then, sweetly, sadly. She reached out a hand and lightly touched my arm, then drew it back.

"Oh, Gaia," she said. "Don't you recognize your own *little sister*, even after all this time?"

19

I gaped at Luna as the coffee bubbled and hissed down into the pot. The words she'd just said seemed utterly unreal to me, like some kind of gibberish in a dream.

"Sister?" I scowled at her. "But I don't *have* a sister."

"You've *always* had one," said Luna. "We've just been—*distant* –for a while."

My scowl deepened. "I don't *remember* having a sister."

"I know," said Luna. "I think there's something wrong with your memory."

The coffeemaker bubbled louder as it neared the end of its cycle. "Your powers." Things were coming together in my mind. "Are they...are you...like me?"

Luna nodded. "You're of the Earth. I'm of...somewhere else."

I frowned. "You're Landkind, then?"

"No," said Luna. "I'm the manifestation of a *world*, as you are. A *different* world." She smiled and pointed upward. "Your *sister* world, in so very many ways."

"The *moon?*" I stared at her in disbelief—though what she was telling me was no more incredible than so much else in my life. "You're trying to tell me you're *the moon?*"

She nodded. "The one and only."

My frown deepened. If what she was telling me was true, I should have remembered it. Between Luna and the Ellie Grenoble's scrapbooks, I was starting to think my memories had been tampered with. "So what happened? Why have you only come back to me now?"

"We grew apart." She shrugged. "We had a falling out. I came back because I needed you...only now I realize you need *me* more."

Mystified, I gazed at her, searching for some kind of sisterly feeling that might be lost deep inside me. But I found nothing. If we shared the connection she was talking about, I had no recollection of it on any level.

But that didn't mean *everyone* in my orbit was just as in the dark about it.

"Duke knew, didn't he?" I asked. "That's why he hired you."

Luna nodded. "We share a special bond. In his way, he's a moon of yours, too."

Talking about Duke brought me back to the emergency at hand. "Where is he, anyway? We need all hands on deck right now."

"I can't say."

"We *need* him here, Luna," I insisted. "We are *way* past the point of the proverbial shit hitting the fan."

"But he asked me not to tell anyone. I have to respect his privacy."

"Can you call him?"

Luna winced. "No phone, he said."

"Uh-huh." I moved closer and slid an arm around her shoulders. "So tell me, did I ever bully you when we were growing up? I forget."

"Not really."

"Well, there's a first time for everything." I squeezed her shoulders just hard enough to make her take notice. "Where the hell is he, sis?"

***

Music filled the night, emanating from the old gray barn as I approached it. Not just any music, either, but the *great* stuff, sweet and familiar as it flowed into my ears.

Big band music.

If only my situation had been less dire, I might have enjoyed it.

Instead, as I walked from my Highlander, all I felt was dark urgency. Driving fifteen minutes into the woods outside town had already taken too long in a time of crisis. I had to get Duke back on deck with no further delay.

Face it, he's my *rock*. And yes, I'm aware of the irony, since rock—or dirt and mud, at least—is what he's made of.

I reached for the handle of the barn door, and then I paused. The song playing inside was one of my favorites, "Jeep's Blues," and the lovely, gliding saxophone solo was in progress.

Yes, I know and love everything Duke Ellington and his band ever wrote. It probably helped that I learned it from the best possible source—Duke himself.

Pulling the big door open, I finally saw where my personal moon had gone. A full-size big band was playing on risers along the far wall, their brass instruments gleaming in the bright light of bulbs swinging from the rafters.

There in the middle of it all, with his back to me, Duke was conducting the orchestra with graceful, looping sweeps of a baton.

The musicians were a mix of ages, races, and genders. There were fifteen of them, all dressed casually in everything from polos and khakis to t-shirts and shorts. Without fail, they played with the smooth precision of a well-oiled group, as if they'd been together for many years.

I let the song play a little longer, though I knew I shouldn't—savored the bluesy swing and slow build of the horns, the hiss of the high-hat cymbals, the tinkling of the keys. For a moment, it could have been 1956, with Duke in his comeback prime and the whole world purring at his doorstep, begging for more.

Then, when the song was over, I applauded, breaking the spell.

Duke turned, and the look on his face said it all. He looked like a kid caught with his hand in a candy jar—surprised, disappointed, and annoyed all at once.

"Hi, Duke." I waved at the band. "Hi, everybody."

They all said hi and waved back.

"So sorry for interrupting," I told them, "but this is pretty important. There's an emergency."

The tone of the musicians changed instantly to one of great concern.

"Excuse me, friends." Duke put his baton on the music stand he'd been using and walked over, taking me aside. "Hello, Gaia." He lowered his voice. "I guess I can't trust that Luna after all, can I?"

I kept my voice to a whisper, too. "First of all, great band," I said. "You've still got it, Duke."

He managed a gracious nod at that. "We call ourselves the Strayhorns. Catchy, isn't it?"

"Second of all, what are you doing with a band *at all?*" I asked. "We *talked* about this. You're a *golem*. No *comebacks*, remember? We have to keep the truth about you a *secret.*"

"It's for a benefit concert," said Duke. "For a very worthy cause."

I frowned. "What cause is that?"

"We're raising money for the family of a terminally ill musician," explained Duke. "He has three children, and the medical bills will leave his wife penniless."

My annoyance was quickly fading. "Well, good for you."

"The concert's in two weeks. I know things have been stressful at the office lately, but I thought, with Luna holding down the fort, I could still get the band ready in time."

As always, Duke's heart was in the right place. "I understand, and you're right," I told him. "We can have an exception to the no comebacks rule for a worthy cause like this—assuming you don't bill yourself as the resurrected *you-know-who.*"

"I wouldn't dream of it, Earth Angel." He smiled.

"However," I said, "I really do *need* you, Duke. *Right now.* It's a five-alarm fire."

The look on his face turned grim. "No fatalities, I trust?"

"Not yet," I said, "but our back room is full of ticking time bombs. I need *you* to help me figure out how to defuse them."

Duke nodded. "Of course."

"And did I mention my *powers* are on the fritz? Only after I helped *destroy* a fracking site?"

Duke blew his breath out in a long exhalation of resignation. "Say no more." He turned to the band on the risers and drew his hand across his neck in a throat-cutting gesture. "We're done for tonight, gang. See you next time."

2 0

<hr>

"We need Veritas." Duke came up with that idea thirty seconds after I told him about Phaola, Blue Knob, and Prince Gallitzin State Park. "Goddess of truth. I'd bet good money she could get through to them."

Now do you see why I need Duke on deck at times like this? We were driving back from the Big Band Barn, and he just pulled a plan out of thin air like *that*. I know he chafes at his life as a golem sometimes, but I *swear* I'd be lost without him.

"Does she live around here?" I asked. As small as it was, Confluence had become a real nexus of supernatural beings—gods and goddesses especially. It was mostly because they wanted to be close to Mother Earth's avatar—at least that was Duke's theory.

"Quite the opposite, I'm afraid," said Duke. "But silver-tongued devil that I am, I believe I might be able to persuade the good woman to grace us with her presence—in a manner of speaking."

I flashed him a look from behind the wheel. "Will she or won't she?" I asked. "Grace us with her presence, that is."

Duke squirmed in his seat and stared out the side window. "We haven't always seen eye to eye on things," he said. "You know how it is. But I do feel strongly that she will come around in support of our very just cause."

"I hope you're right," I said. "The only way we can help our friends is if we understand what's been done to them."

105

"I can tell you this much," said Duke. "Dear Veritas will experience my concerns front and center. They will be *most* prominent in her mind."

His comments sounded ominous, but I had too much else on my mind and let them pass. "I'm worried, Duke," I told him as we rolled through the night toward Confluence. "All this craziness all of a sudden. If it's connected, I hate to think what it might be building up to."

"Nothing you can't handle." Duke reached over and patted my shoulder. "Nothing *we* can't handle."

"Do you think it could be Atlantis again? That he might not have died after all? Or someone from Groundswell, maybe?"

"Too soon to say, Earth Angel." He patted my shoulder again. "Maybe you're not their primary target at all."

He was right; it was possible. Each threat had come when I'd been with somebody else—one person in particular. "You think they're after Ashanti?"

Duke shrugged. "Maybe they want to finish what they started with her, whatever that is...and whoever *they* are."

"I won't let them," I said firmly. "Assuming there's anything I can *do* about it, with these glitchy powers of mine."

"How are they right now?" asked Duke. "Are you getting any signal at all?"

Normally, driving down the road at sixty miles an hour, I could still feel the Earth around me—even manipulate pieces of it as I raced past. On a good day, I could grab gravel from the berm and toss it far, firing it like bullets at a bad guy's car. I'd even been known to trip a tremor en route, setting off a targeted quake in my wake. But with my powers on the blink since the Battle of Shawnee, I wasn't holding out hope for results like those.

I decided to start small, reaching for a clod of dirt from the side of the road. At first, though, I couldn't focus in on that level of detail; all I sensed were the vague contours of the landscape, blurred with the speed of my passage.

Frustrated, I clenched my teeth and concentrated harder, straining to blow away the fog that was blocking me. If anything, the scenery got blurrier. I started to panic that my link to the world had been severed completely and for good.

Then, I felt Duke's hand squeeze my shoulder. "Relax, Earth Angel," he said. "Let it come to you."

"But it's *gone.* I'm *cut off* from the *world.*"

"That's impossible, don't you see?" Duke chuckled. "You *are* the world."

I did what he said, trying to relax instead of fighting to make contact. At first, my perceptions were unchanged.

Then, unexpectedly, the landscape around us burst to life in high relief before my mind's eye. Gasping with surprise and joy, I peered into the manifold layers of the glorious world around us, feeling planet Earth in all its complexity.

"You got there, didn't you?" Again, Duke chuckled. "Good for you."

"The signal is *strong,*" I told him, and then I reached for a clod of dirt. Instead, a *blanket* of the stuff peeled up from the ground and soared out in front of us, rippling in midair like a flying carpet.

"Well done, Earth Angel." Duke patted my shoulder once more before letting go. "The power loss must have been temporary."

"Thank God," I said, grinning at the magic carpet of dirt flowing ahead of us. But even as I said it, I couldn't help wondering.

What if I lost it again at the worst possible moment?

"You were right to bring me in," said Duke as he stared down at the three bodies on the floor of the back room. "This is indeed a most inauspicious situation."

"You're not angry, then?" Luna, who was standing in the doorway to the office area, looked worried. "It's okay that I told them where you were?"

"Under other circumstances, I would be most perturbed." Duke smiled and winked at her. "But in the case at hand, you clearly did the right thing, my dear."

All of us were in the back room at that point, standing around Phaola and the others. I, for one, felt a little better than before—headache gone, powers restored, coffee onboard, Duke at my side. Maybe we were even on the verge of getting answers to some of our questions.

"So how do we contact Veritas?" I asked. "And how do we get her here if she's located far away?"

"The answer to your first question is rather mundane, I'm afraid." With a flourish, Duke pulled a cell phone out of his pants pocket. "A little *modern-day* magic ought to do the trick." Clearing his throat, he thumbed through his contacts, then selected an entry and opened a text window for it. "This is where all that ivory-tinkling finally pays off," he said, rapidly thumb-typing a message onto the screen.

As the rest of us watched, Duke finished his message and hit the send button. A reply came a moment later, leading him to rattle off a reply of his own.

It went like this, back and forth, for several minutes. Some of the replies made Duke chuckle; some made him scowl. One made him shake his head, and another made him curse under his breath.

Then, finally, he looked up at the rest of us arranged around him and nodded. "We're all set."

"Set for what?" I asked. "How's this going to work?"

"Will she just—*zap* herself here?" asked Ashanti.

"Not quite." Duke took off his sweater and unbuttoned his shirt. "It's rather more—*involved*—than that." He pulled off the shirt, revealing a ribbed white scoop-necked t-shirt underneath. "It's more of a **person to person** kind of thing, really."

Duke reached into his pants pockets and fished around for a moment, then pulled out a gold amulet that fit snugly in the palm of his hand. The amulet was round and embossed with an image of a pair of wings.

Duke chanted and passed his hand over them, and the wings started to glow. The glow grew brighter and brighter, pulsing like the beat of a heart.

Then, Duke himself started to glow. A soft light suffused his brown skin, pulsing in time with the brighter light of the amulet. Still, he remained focused on the object in his hand and continued to chant in a language I couldn't remember ever hearing before.

The chanting got louder and faster, and he clamped his eyes shut. The aura around him rippled, and it almost looked to me like his *skin* was rippling, too.

Because it was. As Ashanti, Luna, and I watched, Duke's own physical body began to change. The flesh of his arms and chest and shoulders crawled, as if something were squirming beneath it. That flesh turned pliant and took on a rubbery consistency, then altered again, looking more and more like *clay.*

The very clay I'd used to mold him in the first place, years ago.

Ashanti choked and turned away, but I couldn't blame her. I could see how it might be hard to watch the golem revert to his base ingredients—especially when his face began to melt.

Duke's features ran like those of a waxwork dummy in a fire.

Still, he kept chanting, even as he became increasingly unrecognizable to us.

Then, the process paused—and moved in reverse. The molten flesh flowed back into human features and parts, rippling into the shape of a person again.

But the person wasn't Duke.

It wasn't even a *man*. The body took on a distinctly feminine form, complete with a narrower torso, flared hips, and bulging bustline. The skin changed color from chestnut brown to pale pink, and the hair swelled into ample curls and converted from jet black to glossy red.

As for the face, it became more oval, with bright green eyes instead of brown. The broad nose narrowed, the lips became more full, the age lines and eye bags smoothed. The cheeks hollowed, and the cheekbones became more prominent. The chin rose and tightened, the neck narrowed, the Adam's apple disappeared.

Soon, we were face-to-face with a beautiful, red-haired woman where Duke had once stood. Duke had reshaped his own malleable body to allow her to recreate herself far from home.

Even the voice belonged to her, higher-pitched and feminine as she continued the chant.

Then she stopped chanting and waving her hand over the winged amulet. The aura around her flickered and faded, and the flow of the amulet died out, too.

Duke was gone. In his place stood the goddess of truth, transmitted as if by magic through the ley lines of the Earth.

"Hello, everyone." She smiled at each of us in turn, then lowered her gaze to the bodies on the floor. "And these must be the subjects I've been brought here to examine."

"They are," I told her. "We're not sure what's been done to them, but they're definitely not themselves anymore. They tried to *kill* us when we went to rescue them."

"Do you know who *did* this to them?" asked Veritas.

"Not really," I said. "We found them at a fracking site operated by EarthSave Unlimited, and they attacked us. That pretty much covers everything we know."

"Your honesty is clear to me." Veritas nodded and rubbed her hands together. "It could be any number of things, then. I'll have to interrogate one of them to get at the truth."

"So we'll have to wake one of them up," I said.

"That's usually the first step in questioning, yes." Veritas smirked, but it didn't come across as mean-spirited. I liked her automatically, in fact, though she was very all-business and not so much focused on the feels. I was glad about that, since likeability wasn't always a trait of your average god or goddess on the street.

"Can you do it?" I turned to Luna. "Can you wake up Phaola?" Of the three of them, I wanted to talk to Phaola most; I trusted her and her eye for detail more than anyone in the room.

Luna looked worried. "Are you sure that's what you want me to do? If I wake her in her current condition, she's likely to pick up where she left off and lash out with her powers against us."

"Wake her up just a little, then," said Veritas. "Just enough to answer questions. Keep her in a twilight state the whole time."

Luna frowned, tapping her upper lip with her forefinger. "I haven't tried that before, keeping someone half-awake and half-asleep at the same time."

I held out a fist and smiled. "I have faith in you. I know you can do it."

She stared at my fist for a moment, then bumped it with one of her own. "All right, I'll try."

"Good," I said. "And Ashanti and I will be on alert if she comes to all the way." I looked at Ashanti, and she nodded, her face and posture free of doubt.

I, on the other hand, was *full* of doubt. If Phaola regained full consciousness and control of her powers in her hostile state, she could devastate the offices and everyone in them in short order.

Luna knelt beside Phaola and carefully placed the fingers of one hand on her forehead. She closed her eyes, then, and her own head lowered.

The rest of us stood and watched for long moments without a sign. Only when Luna finally looked up and nodded did I realize I'd been holding my breath the whole time.

Veritas knelt on the opposite side of Phaola from Luna and leaned in close. "Hello, Phaola," she said softly. "Can you hear me?"

Slowly, Phaola's eyes slid open, but she only stared at the ceiling, not the women on either side of her. "No." Her voice was a whisper, just loud enough for Ashanti and I to hear. "I am not Phaola."

Strangely, her lips kept moving after that, but no audible sound came out. The movements could have represented words, I thought, or just involuntary twitches of her mouth.

Veritas frowned and leaned closer. As she did, Phaola's lips stopped moving.

"But I am told this body is Phaola's," said Veritas. "You cannot deny this is true."

"The body is no longer hers," said the voice that was coming from Phaola. "Her self has been removed and replaced with mine."

"And who are you?"

Phaola shook her head. "You won't get that information out of me."

"At least tell me how she was removed and replaced," said Veritas.

"First, The Hollowing," said Phaola. "Then, The Filling."

"And how exactly are those things done?"

"The magic of the land," said Phaola, "and the science of man, united. Ultimate power wielded by those who would serve the greater good."

"Who are they?" asked Veritas. "Who wields the power?"

"That information is on a need-to-know basis." Phaola's sneer was cruel, not at all like her. "And *you* do not need to know...*yet*."

Veritas looked frustrated...until Phaola's lips again moved silently, as before. The goddess of truth in the body of Duke watched them carefully, reading what they were saying. I tried to do the same, but lip-reading is something I've never been good at.

"I see," Veritas said after a moment. "So *that's* who's controlling all this."

Phaola's brow knitted with annoyance. "What are you talking about? I said *nothing* about those in control."

"Shhh," said Veritas. "I'm talking to Phaola, not you."

Phaola's voice rose to an angry shout. *"I told you, Phaola's gone! It's just me in here now!"*

"That's a lie," said Veritas. "The Hollowing was imperfect. Phaola's self is as present as yours within that form. I know because she *told* me so."

My heart beat faster at the hope that my friend was still alive in that body, that perhaps we could somehow yet save her.

Or, maybe, she could still find a way to save herself.

"Tell me more, Phaola." Veritas was still intently focused on my friend inside that body. "Tell me *why*. Why are they *doing* this?"

"No!" shouted the dominant voice I now knew was not truly Phaola's. "You get *nothing!* Nothing until it's *too late!*"

Seconds later, Phaola's lips again moved silently. Veritas stayed close and tracked every word they uttered, watching every syllable they shaped. With every fiber of my being, I wanted to know what those syllables were.

"Tell me more," said Veritas. "Tell me what they're planning. What's happening next?"

Phaola's lips moved some more, and Veritas nodded grimly.

"And when will that happen?" she asked.

This time, even I could read the latest word on Phaola's lips. It reached me loud and clear.

Tomorrow.

Whatever terrible thing was coming, it would happen tomorrow.

"Tell me more, Phaola," said Veritas.

"You're doomed!" howled whoever had tried to replace her, whose voice was so much louder than her own now. "*Gaia Charmer*, you are *doomed!*"

"Tell me everything, Phaola." Veritas pressed her fingers to the side of Phaola's head, and the howling voice screamed in pain. "Tell me the *truth* and nothing *but* the truth...and I will lead you to the *true light* as you do it."

"There." Veritas withdrew her hands from Phaola's head and leaned back on her heels. "I have done all that I can for her. She needs to rest again."

At a nod from Veritas, Luna fluttered her fingers, and Phaola settled back into a deep sleep.

I stared down at Phaola's face. She looked serene, though the invader of her body had fought and screamed throughout Veritas' treatment. "Is she all right? Did you manage to bring her original self back to the forefront?"

Veritas looked weary and let out a long sigh. "I tried to bring out as much of her as remained inside this body, but we won't know for sure until she wakes up. I won't lie to you. She was traumatized and buried deep."

Ashanti moved forward and touched Veritas' shoulder. "What about me?" she asked. "Do you think *my* original self is still buried in *here*?" She touched her chest with the splayed fingers of her right hand. "Do you think you could bring it out as well?"

"Let's see how Phaola fares first," said Veritas. "Then we'll move on to you and the other Landkinders...or at least as many of you as we can in the time remaining."

I was alarmed at what she'd said. "So our time is limited, then? Something's going to happen?"

Nodding slowly, Veritas got to her feet. "The enemy is coming.

Those who made *her* what she is..." She gestured at Phaola. "Those who did *all* of this to your friends...they *are* coming. And very soon."

I frowned, feeling a swell of deep foreboding. "Who are they? What do they want?"

Veritas slumped, looking more tired by the minute. "Do you have coffee? I need something right now."

"This way." I led her into the front office, where the half-full coffee pot was still on the warmer.

I grabbed one of the plain white guest mugs stacked on the counter and filled it with steaming black liquid, then put it down in front of her.

"So who are they?" I asked. "Who are the people behind what happened to Phaola?"

I noticed, as Veritas emptied a packet of artificial sweetener into the mug, that her hands were shaking. The work she'd done with Phaola must've taken more out of her than I'd realized.

"The government," she said grimly. "*Your* government." She stirred in the sweetener, added a single creamer, and raised the mug toward her lips. "They're engaged in a project to neutralize the forces of Landkind, which they see as a threat." She had a long sip of the coffee and looked grateful for it. "They see them also as a powerful *weapon*."

I stroked my braid thoughtfully. Weaponizing Landkind was *not* a new idea. It had been one of the chief strategies of Groundswell during its heyday, back before my friends and I had put an end to it. "So they know about Groundswell?"

"According to Phaola, they do." Veritas had another sip of coffee. "What happened at Parapets terrified them. They were determined never to let Landkind threaten the nation's security again. The best way to do that, they decided, was to take *control* of Landkind."

"But that kind of geomantic manipulation..."

"...was not beyond the capabilities of Groundswell, was it?" said Veritas. "Your government retrieved and recruited some of the best minds from Parapets and put them to work on this project, which they call Terralyze. They figured out a process, which they called The Hollowing, to separate the minds of Land-kind from their bodies. Then, they developed another process, The

Filling, to implant their own hand-picked military personnel into the emptied bodies and put them to work in the service of their masters."

"They want to use Landkind to fight their wars?" I said. "Typical." The thought of it made me furious. Humans, for all their potential for goodness, so often were obsessed with murdering their own kind, destroying their own environment, and using whatever they could find to cause the most destruction and chaos.

"That's not their only goal, however," said Veritas. "They have a *much* more terrible plan in mind."

By now, Luna and Ashanti had drifted into the front office area and were listening to our conversation.

"What could *be* more terrible?" asked Luna.

"Controlling Landkind has its limits," explained Veritas. "America's leaders want to go *beyond* those limits. They want to *dominate* the world in *every* way, which is why they are coming for *you*." She jabbed a finger at my chest.

"Me?" I said.

Veritas nodded. "That is true. Phaola told me so herself."

"That's what Phaola meant when she said Gaia was doomed?" asked Ashanti.

Veritas nodded. "Even as we speak, the government's forces are on their way. They plan to take you in the morning." Again, she pointed at me. "They intend to replace your mind with that of one of their agents."

"How is that even possible?" I was staggered, unable to believe what I was hearing. My stomach churned, and my head throbbed. "I should have *sensed* it before now. I should have *known* this was coming."

Veritas reached out and touched my upper arm. "I will tell you *one more true thing* before I try to help the others," she said. "You have strayed from your *self*, Gaia Charmer...from your *truth*...and from your *reason for being*. That you now face a battle for your own survival...that is the price you must pay for your negligence."

Recognizing the truth of her words, I hung my head. I couldn't deny that I'd avoided my duties as Mother Earth, that I'd failed to embrace my role fully. But it was just so *big*, so hard to wrap my head around; it had been easier to stay in my comfortable little life as Gaia the private eye, Gaia the girlfriend, Gaia the only-slightly-above-average.

And Veritas knew it without the slightest iota of doubt. She could see right through me, just as she could see through everyone and everything else.

"However," she continued, "it is not too late for you. All the power of all the world is at your fingertips, everywhere, always. Open yourself to the possibilities, and you will be *unstoppable.*"

I nodded as if I understood completely, as if what she'd just told me were obvious and simple to grasp...but I felt no more enlightened than before.

Veritas had another drink of coffee and put the mug back down on the counter. "All that I have told you is true."

Then she turned and walked to the back room, leaving me stunned and ashamed in her wake, wondering what to do next.

And hurt, most of all, by the fact that I *knew* everything she had told me was true.

"It's the *government*," shouted Minthe as she burst into the office. "Oh my gods, it's the *government*."

Nephelae followed her in and nodded, holding up a printed sheet of paper. "What *she* said."

The two of them had hammered on the front door until I'd unlocked it and let them in. Now that they'd made their big announcement, I hated to tell them Phaola had already spoiled it.

Veritas, ever a blunt speaker of the unvarnished truth, had no such compunction. "We already *know* all that," she said, "but how do *you*, whoever you are?"

The two nymphs glared at her, annoyed that she'd stolen their thunder.

Clearly, it was time for me to intervene. "Veritas, allow me to introduce Minthe and Nephelae. They are two of my best customers and also two of my best friends."

"Hello." Veritas nodded stiffly. "Always good to see nymphs like you at large in the modern world."

"You know we're nymphs?" snapped Minthe.

"That truth, at least, is obvious," said Veritas.

I cleared my throat to finish the introductions. "Minthe and Nephelae, meet Veritas, goddess of truth. We brought her in to consult on a case—a *different* case—but maybe they've both ended up at the same place. What was it you were saying about the government, Minthe?"

"We finished examining the sample of ash from the fire-breathing cloud," said Minthe. "It took a *long* time and a lot of work."

Nephelae nodded. "We used every kind of magic at our disposal, Gaia. We even brought in friends with more—*scientific*—expertise."

"*Discreetly,*" said Minthe. "We brought them in *discreetly*. We remembered you said to be careful."

"Minthe and I were able to tell that the ash wasn't from a demon or a dragon or an ifrit," said Nephelae. "We knew it was man-made...and our friends told us *which* men had made it."

"The U.S. government, that's who." Minthe looked disgusted. "The chemical composition of the ash matches the skin of certain U.S. military-grade *drones*."

"And it's saturated with a *napalm*-like chemical used in some *flamethrowers,*" added Nephelae.

"Mystery solved!" Minthe laughed. "You and Ashanti weren't attacked by a fire-breathing creature at all."

"It was a flamethrowing government drone," added Nephelae.

I nodded. What they'd told us lined up with what we already knew...but it changed nothing. If what Phaola had told us was as true as Veritas thought, the forces of human darkness would attack in the morning, and they wouldn't be deterred.

"Thank for the information," I said finally. "Now you should both get going. I'll call if we need anything else."

Minthe frowned. "You're giving us the bum's rush?"

"Don't take it personally," I said. "In fact, I want *all* of you to clear out. It's been a tough day, and I still have a shit-ton of work to do."

Everyone just stood around and exchanged looks, the exact opposite of what I'd just told them to do.

"Go on." I marched over to the door, swung it wide, and gestured at the open doorway. "There's no use in *none* of us getting any sleep."

"But the government's coming for you in the morning," said Ashanti. "Phaola said you're *doomed.*"

"Wait, what?" Minthe sounded alarmed. "You didn't *mention*..."

"That's why she's trying to get rid of us," Veritas said with the absolute certainty of a truth-teller. "She wants us out of the line of fire if fighting breaks out."

"Like that's going to happen." Ashanti smacked her fist in the palm of her hand, sending sparks spitting through the air of the office. "I, for one, am not going anywhere."

"Neither am I," said Nephelae.

"That goes for both of us." Minthe laughed. "Never let it be said that nymphs like us won't stand up for our beloved Mother Earth."

"Everyone, please." Again, I gestured at the doorway. I wished they'd all listen to me for once, especially now that so much danger was on the way. "I promise, I can handle this."

"Not if your power fluctuations continue," said Ashanti.

"She speaks the truth," said Veritas.

"Who asked you?" I snapped. "I'm the one who *invited* you here, remember?"

With that, Luna stepped forward, coming face-to-face with me. "Gaia," she said firmly. "I speak for us *all* when I say *none* of us are going to abandon you in your hour of need."

Veritas cleared her throat. "Actually, I need to get going. I have other commitments I need to return to, and..."

"None of us but *her* are going to abandon you," corrected Luna. "Just as we know *you* would never abandon *us.*"

I looked around at them, feeling annoyed...also feeling *worried* about what might happen to them if they stayed. But at the same time, I felt something else, too, something that made my heart beat faster in my chest.

Honored. Loved. *Hopeful*. I felt all those things.

As dark as tomorrow looked from where I stood, perhaps there was hope for salvation if all these people cared enough to fight at my side.

Not that I was going to tell *them* that. "Have it your way." I shut the door and glared around the room, doing my best to look displeased. "But don't come crying to me when the government tears you all a new one."

"We wouldn't dream of it, boss." Luna was all smiles. "And

anyway, it won't happen like that, and you know it. We're *going* to win."

I met Veritas' gaze. "Are we?"

She just shrugged. "How the hell should I know? Do I *look* like the Oracle at Delphi?" And then she marched into the back room while the rest of us laughed.

I wiped a tear from my cheek when Phaola's eyes fluttered open and fixed on me.

"Gaia!" It was *her* voice speaking from those lips, not the voice of whoever had been implanted in her head by the government. "I'm back!"

"I'm so glad," I told her, dabbing away another tear. "I've been so *worried* about you, my friend."

"She's not out of the woods yet." Veritas was kneeling with Phaola's head in her lap, massaging her temples after administering the last round of treatment. "The other mind still infects her, though I've pushed it to the background."

"She's in charge again," I said, patting Phaola's arm.

"But she might not stay that way," said Veritas. "She still has a fight on her hands, I'm afraid."

"I can handle it, now that you've given me a fighting chance." Phaola nodded. "I'll rip that *asshole* right out of my cerebrum and kick him to the *curb.*"

"I believe you just might." Veritas looked at the other two Land-kind bodies stretched out on the floor of the back room. "But I'm not so sure about the others."

"Give them more of the same treatment you gave me," said Phaola. "Blue Knob Mountain and Prince Gallitzin State Park are pretty tough, you know."

"The minds possessing them are more tenacious than the one that took you over, Phaola." With that, Veritas turned to meet my gaze. "I'd think twice before waking them. If you *do* wake them, watch out for unusual behavior." She dipped her gaze, and I realized she was referring to Phaola, too. "You can't be too careful."

Message received. "Thanks for doing your best with them," I told her. "Could you take a look at Ashanti, too, before you go?"

"Of course." Veritas gently lifted Phaola's head from her lap and got to her feet. "But I can only spare a minute or two."

As Veritas headed into the front office to find Ashanti, Phaola pushed herself to a sitting position and smiled. "Sorry I tried to kill you at the fracking site, girlfriend," she told me. "I wasn't myself."

"I know," I said. "And I'm sorry Luna kicked your ass there, too."

"Who's Luna? Have we met?"

I shrugged. "You were out cold the whole time. But you didn't miss much. She's nothing to write home about. Just, you know, the *human avatar* of the freakin' *moon.*"

Phaola grinned. "Sorry I missed her."

"And I'm sorry I didn't come for you sooner." I knew it was a buzzkill thing to say, but it was something I needed to put out there. "I'm sorry I didn't know you were in danger sooner."

"Stop that." Phaola touched my cheek. "I could've called you any time. *I* was the one who decided to march in there without asking for help from my friend the *entire planet.*"

"Well, I haven't been a very *good* planet lately," I told her. "I didn't even *notice* a government conspiracy was abducting and reprogramming *Landkind* across the country."

"So you're telling me big, bad Mother Earth isn't perfect? Well, hot damn!" She grinned. "I guess you're more *human* than you *thought.*"

I shook my head. "No, I'm serious, Phae. I've been wrapped up in my own shit, and I let everyone down. Now all hell's about to break loose."

"Hey." She squeezed my shoulder. "You're not the one who kidnapped all those Landkinders, hollowed them out, and put soldiers' minds in charge of their bodies, are you?"

"No, but..."

"No buts." Phaola squeezed tighter. "You are *not* the bad guy here. Neither am I, though I do have one taking up space in my brain."

Phaola had a way of always making me feel better—but I was still worried about her. "Are you going to be okay?" I asked. "Are you sure you can manage the creep in your head?"

She gave me a steady-eyed stare of great sincerity. "Absolutely, Gaia. But if I have the slightest doubt whatsoever at any time, you'll be the first to know."

"Because you'll try to kill me?"

"Because I'll give you a heads-up before I go sideways. I *promise*. And I give you permission in advance to leave the kid gloves off. Don't hold back, if it comes to it. Okay?"

I nodded, though I had zero intention of keeping that promise. Sacrificing a friend, knowingly, was right at the top of the list of things I would *never* do.

When Phaola and I walked back into the office, Ashanti was in a chair with her head tipped back and her eyes closed. Veritas stood over her, fingers pressed to Ashanti's temples, gazing with intense focus at her face.

Luna looked our way and raised a finger to her lips. Minthe and Nephelae didn't even notice us; they were too wrapped up in watching whatever Veritas was doing to Ashanti.

"Try once more to remember," Veritas said softly. "We know you are the Great Lady of the Grand Canyon. Tell us what you recall of your life in that role."

Ashanti scowled. "Nothing. It's all a blank. It's like I never existed until Phaola found me wandering in the woods."

"Relax," said Veritas. "Think back. Let yourself drift on the current of the past."

Ashanti's brow softened. "All right. I'll let myself drift."

"Float back...back. Take a deep breath and slowly release it."

Ashanti's chest rose as she inhaled deeply...then compressed as she let the breath out. Again, she did the same, and again after that.

"Look around, Ashanti," said Veritas. "What do you see?"

"I see...I see..." Suddenly, her face twisted, she let out a sob. She lurched up, grabbing for Veritas, and pulled her close, crying into her shoulder. "I don't see *anything*. Just *darkness*."

"That's all right." Veritas rubbed her back soothingly, looking in my direction. "You'll be all right." Meeting my gaze, she shook her head slowly, telling me everything I needed to know about Ashanti's condition.

Her memory was not coming back anytime soon.

When Ashanti was done crying, Veritas said her goodbyes. She'd return if we needed her, she said, but for now it was time to go.

"Thanks for the coffee." She shook my hand. "I've enjoyed meeting you—the latest *incarnation* of you, that is."

"You've met others?" I asked. "Other incarnations?"

Veritas grinned. "I've met them *all.*"

"Could you tell me about them?"

"Someday." Veritas winked. "If you live through what's coming in the morning."

Then, with a jaunty wave to everyone, she went in the back room and shut the door. Apparently, she wanted a little privacy when she went through her transformation back into Duke.

The rest of us watched her go, then stood around staring at each other—but the awkward moment didn't last. It couldn't have been more than thirty seconds later that a knock pounded the front door.

I walked over and peeked out from the edge of the blinds...then unlocked and opened the door without further hesitation. Of all the people I wanted to see just then, he was at the top of the list.

"Hi, Gaia." Briar nodded at me as he entered the place, then looked around and nodded at the others, as well. "Ladies."

"What's up, Dale?" I asked. "Do you need something?"

He shook his head grimly. "I'm here to help. I heard things are about to go off the rails in a big way."

"How did you hear that?" I turned in time to see Luna hastily shove her phone in her pocket, trying to look innocent. "Never mind."

Agitated, Briar took my arm. "Let's get you out of here, Gaia."

"No," snapped Phaola. "It'll just make it worse."

Everyone looked at her at once. Was her hostile inner passenger doing the talking again?

"Seriously, Gaia," said Phaola. "They're coming *here* whether *you're* here or not. If you hide somewhere, they'll punish everyone else they can find. They'll destroy the whole *town*."

Briar frowned at her, looking confused. He knew her well, since she was such a good friend of mine, but what she said just wasn't tracking. "What the hell is going on here? Since when does *Phaola* know the bad guys' evil plans?"

"Since a bad guy took up residence in her *head*," said Nephelae.

"Not that he's in *control* anymore," added Minthe.

"We don't *think*," said Nephelae.

Briar looked around at each of us, taking in what he'd just heard, trying to process it. Then, he threw his arms in the air with a flourish. "Whatever you guys say." After being a part of my world for so long, he knew better than to keep asking questions when dramatic license was clearly called for. "So this office is where we make our stand, correct?"

"There's no 'we' in this, Dale," I told him. "Unpowered individuals should be as far from here as possible. That goes for townspeople, which is where you come in. I want you to evacuate the local civilians and close all the streets around this building."

"Sure, no problem," he replied. "And if they ask why I just woke them out of a sound sleep and told them to get out?"

"You could say there's a gas leak," I suggested. "That would be a good explanation for the street closures, too."

"And then you want me out of the way while you fight for your life," Briar said with a tinge of anger. "Is that it? Did I cover everything?"

I didn't expect the pushback. "Dale, I just..."

"Well, you can forget it, Gaia," snapped Briar. "I'll evacuate people and close streets, but there's *no way* I'll make *myself* scarce when the woman I *love* is in *danger*."

"But, Dale—"

"Is that *clear*?"

"Clear as day, Sheriff," said Luna.

"Couldn't be clearer," agreed Minthe.

"Roger that," said Nephelae.

"Good." Briar nodded with satisfaction, looking around the

room, then settling his gaze on mine. "Because that's how it's gotta be."

With that, he spun and crossed the room, making a beeline for the big whiteboard on the far wall. The board was occupied by one big message announcing a sale on Asian adventure trips, and he wiped it clean with an eraser from the tray along its lowermost edge.

"Now who wants to help me map out a battle plan?" Briar put down the eraser, uncapped a black dry-erase marker, and started drawing lines with it.

At that instant, the door to the back room swung open, and Duke marched out, waving a hand in the air. "I do! I do!"

Briar looked at Phaola. "I'm guessing they'll bring more of those mind-controlled Landkind?"

Phaola nodded and tapped the side of her head with a fingertip. "My *other* brain just confirmed it."

"Then we're going to have our hands full." Briar's sketch of the Cruel World/Charmer Investigations building and surrounding neighborhood was taking shape.

"And Gaia's powers have been on the fritz," said Duke.

Briar turned to me, looking surprised. "They have?"

"But they're fine right now," I insisted. "I promise."

"Still." Briar hid the concern in his eyes by turning back to the whiteboard. "We have even more reason to plan accordingly. We need to account for the variables and prepare fallbacks."

"Good thinking." Luna smiled. "It's times like this when it's pretty *awesome* having a boss whose *boyfriend* is a *sheriff*."

"You said it!" said Minthe and Nephelae at the same time, giggling.

I just smiled and let Briar continue planning on the whiteboard. The truth was, he and the others only knew about *some* of the picture. An altogether different plan was taking shape in my mind at the same time, a plan none of them would be privy to until much later. They didn't *need* to be in on it, since none of them would be involved. *I* was the only one who'd be directly at risk, and it would be well worth the gamble.

Because it might just save everyone in the end. It might just stop EarthSave and whatever they threw at us.

But I wouldn't take the chance of sharing it with even my closest allies, because they might try to stop me from going through with it...especially Briar. One way or the other, the secret plan would remain my secret until I followed through with it or died trying.

26

Was it smart of me to stand out on the street alone when I knew an attack force was out there somewhere plotting my capture?

At that particular moment, I didn't care. It was three in the morning, no hostiles seemed to be nearby, and I needed to get some damn fresh air.

The bipolar mood I liked to call "Sinking Fast" had me locked in its steely clutches and was dragging me down in a hurry. My friends were making plans, preparing for the fight, but as the hours ticked away, I just felt lower and lower.

Whatever was going to happen, I wished with all my heart that I was already on the other side of it. I just wished it could be over, so the *dread* would be over, and I wouldn't have to worry anymore.

Leaning against my parked Highlander, I tipped my head back and gazed up at the dark, cloudy sky between the streetlights. A car hissed past—some local, no doubt, on the way back from a bar—but Confluence was otherwise quiet. It could have been any Saturday night, nothing special about it, not possibly the last night of my life as I knew it. But "Sinking Fast" and I knew better.

It was times like these I sometimes wished I'd taken up smoking.

Just then, the front door of the office opened. I looked, expecting Briar to march out on a safety check.

And surprise—it was Luna instead.

"There you are." She closed the door behind her and joined me in leaning against the Highlander. "Wrapping your head around the incoming shit, I take it?"

"Do you have a cigarette?" I asked her.

She looked at me with a stunned expression. "I didn't know you smoked, sis."

"I don't." I sighed, stroking my braid. "But now seems like a pretty good time to start."

Luna chuckled and bumped me with her elbow. "You're not worried, are you?"

"Mostly that bad things will happen to people I care about," I said.

"You are *literally* the entire *world*," said Luna. "Pretty sure you can *handle* these assholes."

I took a deep breath and let it out slowly. The cool night air felt good as it swirled into and out of my body. "What if I get disconnected from the planet again? What if my powers cut out in the heat of battle?"

"Then you've got the rest of us to back you up," said Luna. "And we will give those shits the fight of their *lives*, believe you me."

I nodded. It was true, I had my team around me—Luna, Briar, Duke, Phaola, Minthe, Nephelae—but I still felt shrouded in darkness. I still felt like I was at the bottom of a deep well without any handholds to climb out again. Even the secret plan I'd concocted seemed doomed to failure.

"I can't let them Hollow and Fill me," I said. "If humankind took over the soul of the Earth, the consequences..." I let the sentence trail away for effect.

Luna moved closer and looped her arm around my own. "It won't come to that, sis. We won't let them hurt you. We won't let them win."

I watched the shadows of my friends shifting across the blinds in the office windows. "If it comes down to it, and I still have control, I'll do *anything* to stop them. Even if it means the *end*."

Luna frowned. "The end of what?"

"*You* know," I said darkly. "The world."

We were both quiet for a long moment. The end I'd mentioned had nothing to do with my secret plan; it wasn't even something I'd consciously thought about before. But now that I'd said it, I realized there was truth to it. It was something I might be willing to do, if things got bad enough.

Somewhere in the distance, a cat screeched three times and fell silent.

Luna hugged me closer. "Don't think like that. Don't give the idea any space in your head."

"It's not my *first* choice, but..."

"Take it from *me*." She stared at me, looking deeply serious. "I know from *experience*. Or have you forgotten how the moon *used* to be?"

I *had* forgotten. Or maybe the knowledge was all there, but I just hadn't looked back that far since regaining my self-awareness. Once again, slacking off in dealing with my heritage had nipped me on the ass.

"You did the same thing?" I asked. "You...destroyed yourself?"

"You should know. You were there." Luna sighed loudly. "And undoing that mistake is why I came back down to Earth in the first place. It's why I came to see you, sis."

"Undoing the mistake?"

"If we get through this," said Luna. "*When* we get through this —I want you to help me be *reborn*. I want you to help bring the *moon* back to *life.*"

I frowned in disbelief. "Is that even possible?"

"I *need* your help, Gaia," said Luna. "To save *my* world and the people who sleep there. How's *that* for giving you motivation to survive?"

Just then, the door swung open, and Briar peered out, looking annoyed. "Care to pitch in on the planning side, you two? We can't do it all ourselves, you know."

"Sure." Luna let go of my arm and strolled inside. "We can't let the Sheriff do *everything,* can we, Gaia?"

I sighed, because I still had about a thousand questions for her— but our private time was over. "No, we can't, Luna." I pushed away from the Highlander and headed for the door. "Everyone *knows* battle plans require a *woman's* touch."

27

Getting some sleep would have been the smart thing to do, but the only ones napping were Blue Knob Mountain and Prince Gallitzin State Park. The rest of us were too busy getting ready for the upcoming battle to feel even the slightest bit sleepy.

We chugged coffee, argued over the battle plan, debated possibilities, and watched the clock. Six a.m., when we would make our first move, would roll around before we knew it.

We did have our share of surprise guests, which helped keep things lively. *Any* guests would have been a surprise at four o'clock on a Sunday morning in Confluence—though these particular guests were especially unexpected.

Mahoney from Doc Yough's came first, offering his services in the forthcoming fight. Apparently, Duke had texted him, calling him in to reinforce our meager battalion.

"I'll gladly fight beside you, Gaia," said Mahoney. "If you'll have me."

Mahoney might have looked like a scrawny, bearded mountain man, but I knew he was a force to be reckoned with. As the avatar of Ohiopyle State Park, he had all the power of the mighty Youghiogheny River at his fingertips, its raging whitewater enough to overcome formidable enemies.

"I'd fight at your side any day of the year, Mahoney." I held him by the arms, then reeled him in for a giant hug. "It would be an *honor*, my friend."

About a half-hour later, something seriously loud pulled up outside, signaling more new arrivals. The knocks on the door that followed sounded like the blows from a jackhammer, hard and fast enough to break right through if I didn't open up quick.

When I threw the door wide, I was totally surprised. Two young people grinned back at me—a redheaded guy and a blonde girl—both of them clad in black leather and armed to the teeth.

"Roy! Rusty!" I couldn't keep the excitement out of my voice. I hadn't seen them much in the past six months, since they'd helped me infiltrate and defeat Groundswell at Parapets in West Virginia. "Long time no see!"

We couldn't hug because of all the guns in the way, but I impulsively hopped forward and pecked each of them on the cheek. Like me, they couldn't stop smiling.

"Two recruits for the Charmer Militia, ma'am!" Roy Price snapped off a crisp salute. "As you can see, we brought plenty of party favors."

"And there're more in the truck." Rusty Quick hiked a thumb at the giant red pickup parked behind them. "Our motto is 'be prepared.' That and, 'It's not nice to fool with Mother Earth.'"

I was so happy to see them—and maybe a little punchy, too, from lack of sleep—that I forgot my worries about bad things happening to the people choosing to fight for me. They might not have been any older than 20 or 21, but they'd been invaluable in my fight with Groundswell, and I knew they'd be helpful again.

"How's Corinne?" I asked, referring to Roy's mother. "How's Late Jim's?" That was the diner she ran in Rough Run, West Virginia. She'd been a waitress there when we'd first met, but she'd taken ownership of the place after the fall of Parapets.

"Both are great, as always," said Roy. "Mom sends her regards, of course. She wanted to come, but she had to stay and take care of my little brother."

"Maybe it's just as well," I said. "This could be a hell of a fight. Duke told you we're going up against the federal government, didn't he?"

"Even better," said Rusty. "Bring 'em on."

"Did he tell you they've taken over some fully-powered Land-kind?" I asked. "It'll be a dangerous showdown, to say the least."

"Dangerous for *them*, you mean." Roy laughed.

"I agree with my man, here," said Rusty. "We're *West Virginians*. Those ass-clowns won't know what *hit* 'em."

Just then, Briar cleared his throat loudly. "It's about that time," he said. "Let's get this show on the road."

Everyone parted to make a path for him to the door, except me. I waited as he approached, my heart pounding in my chest.

"Good luck," I told him.

His gaze locked with mine, sending shivers up my spine. Without a word, he took me by the shoulders and pulled me close.

And then, right there in front of everyone, he gave me a long and loving kiss.

I closed my eyes, savoring the feel of his lips crushed against mine, drinking it in. If things went wrong, I knew, this could be the last kiss we ever shared. It could be the last time we held each other.

Somehow, that made it all the sweeter and more intense. It felt to me as if we were alone together in time and space, with no one else watching or sharing the moment.

I didn't want it to end. My love for him burned like a flame inside me, surging and twisting. I was grateful for every moment I'd spent with him, and I longed for millions more.

"Gaia," he whispered as he pulled away from me. "I have to go. It's six. I have to evacuate and cordon off the area."

"Right." I lingered there for just a moment, afraid to break the spell...afraid, yes, of facing what was to come. Then, slowly, I let go and stepped back. "Stay in touch," I said. "Give us the signal to take our positions."

"You know I will." He unhooked the radio from his belt and handed it to me. "I'll call from the car."

"Okay."

He turned then and whipped open the door. "Let's do this thing." He stepped outside, then ducked back in with one last thing to tell us all. "Any trouble, don't hesitate to call."

"We shall indeed call as needs must, good constable," said Duke.

"Asking only in return that *you* do the same, as we all face this challenge together."

"You bet your ass I will." Briar grinned, shot me a wink, and darted out the door for good this time.

Leaving me standing there, feeling smaller than any woman with a planet for a soul had any right to.

A few minutes after Briar left, there was another knock at the front door. Before anyone could answer it, the handle turned, and the door slammed inward.

Everyone's gaze flew there at the same time as "Caravan" played on the chime. My breath caught in my throat, and I think everyone else's did, too. Was the attack beginning already? We'd thought we'd have more time. *Why didn't we lock the damn door?*

Then, I saw a familiar face and relaxed. What F.B.I. Agent Frank Wagner was doing there at 6:15 in the morning, I didn't know, but at least he wasn't a rampaging, possessed Landkind.

"I *thought* I heard a party going on in here!" Frank chuckled as he let himself in. "But why weren't *we* invited?"

"Maybe they just assumed we'd crash it." Agent Judy Lewis followed him in, grinning and waving a little too merrily for that time of the morning. "In which case, mission accomplished!"

"What's up, you guys?" Immediately, I thought of the battle plan on the whiteboard and the guns all over the place, though it was probably too late to worry about all that now. At least the plan wasn't complete; I'd left off one last resort move that I was keeping to myself.

I pushed forward, hoping I could block the view and ease them back outside...to no avail. Frank and Judy stood squarely in the doorway and wouldn't budge.

"Actually," said Frank, "we were on our way to breakfast, and I thought I'd try one more time to recruit you into federal law enforcement. Though lookie here." He nodded beyond my right shoulder at the whiteboard and guns. "I guess maybe I've been barking up the wrong tree here."

My stomach twisted. This was just the kind of complication we didn't need right now, with the attack about to happen.

"We're into role-playing games," I said, hoping that might be enough to deflect them.

"And guns." Frank smirked.

"They're all registered," said Roy. "We're not breaking any laws."

Frank shook his head. "It doesn't matter, does it?" He glanced at Judy.

"Not one damn bit," said Judy. "When the shit comes down, you'd do just as well with a bunch of squirt guns and cream pies."

A sharp chill shot through my body. A terrible realization crashed into me like an ocean wave I hadn't seen coming.

"But there *is* one thing that *might* work," Judy said slyly. "If you turn yourself in and come with us right now, I think the whole shitshow could be avoided. What do you think, Frank?"

"Sure, why not?" Frank clapped his hands together, then spread them wide. "I'd say that could work out to *everyone's* advantage."

Again, a chill swept through me. Everyone in the room seemed to understand, too, as they were all stone-cold quiet and hanging on every word.

"I see." In retrospect, none of this should have been a surprise. Agent Frank had been lurking around for days, trying to "recruit" me. Phaola had told us the federal government was behind the Landkind takeover scheme. Didn't it make perfect sense that the Federal Bureau of Investigation was involved in the plot to seize control of the world, of me?

"So what do you say, Gaia?" asked Frank. "Shall we bring you aboard Project Terralyze and avoid the unpleasantness?"

Agent Judy nodded encouragingly. "It really is the smart play here, Gaia. I mean, you don't want to see all your friends pay the price for your stubbornness, do you?"

"Besides, you'll be serving your country." Frank smiled and

reached for a handshake. "So what do you say? Want to help defend innocent Americans from terrorist threats to our democracy?"

I thought for a long moment, considering my options. The safety of my friends mattered most to me, but I doubted they'd be any safer if Terralyze managed to hollow out my mind and exert control over the world.

What if I killed their point people, the F.B.I. agents, right there in my office? I was sure I could do it, but I couldn't imagine that would stop the rest of their forces from attacking.

That left one other option, the same one we'd been preparing all night to take, whatever the outcome.

"If I were you, fighting back wouldn't be my first choice," said Frank, as if he could read my mind. "That one over there? With the raging energy blasts?" He pointed at Ashanti. "We've got a small *army* of people with that level of firepower on the way here as we speak."

"They will *slaughter* this ragtag band of misfits you've cobbled together." Judy sneered. "Excuse me, I meant to say *suicidal* misfits."

"Why throw their lives away like that?" asked Frank. "Why not just accept your fate and go with the flow?"

"Free yourself of the responsibility," said Judy. "Stop carrying the weight of the *world* on your shoulders." She chuckled.

I thought about it another moment, then slowly shook my head. "Thanks, but no thanks. If you think I'd ever surrender the Earth to pathetic people like you, you're sadly mistaken."

"Oh, that's too bad." Judy tipped her head to her left shoulder and pooched out her lower lip in feigned disappointment. "You're forcing us to beat the living *shit* out of you."

"Have it your way, Gaia." Grinning cruelly, Frank turned and waggled his fingers in a mocking wave at Ashanti. "You too, sweetheart. Just remember, we offered you the easy way out."

"The *hard* way is our favorite *every time*, though," said Judy. "You'll see!"

"Later, gang!" said Frank as he backed out of the doorway.

"Bye for now!" Judy followed him out and slammed the door behind them.

That left the rest of us standing in the office, shell-shocked, in their wake.

Finally, Minthe cleared her throat. "So I guess we're about to save the world, huh?"

I marched over to the door and locked it, then turned to face my crew. "Anyone who wants out, now's the time. No one will think any less of you. If anything, we'll feel relieved that you'll be safe."

No one took me up on the offer. Every person in the room stood with shoulders squared and jaws clenched, looking defiant.

"All right then." I nodded. "Briar ought to have the streets evacuated and cordoned off by now. I'd say it's time we got out and took up our positions."

"Agreed, Earth Angel. But first, a little sendoff." Duke went to the electronic keyboard set up in the back corner of the room and switched it on. He then proceeded to play something I'd never heard him play before--a jazz piano version of a rock song that instantly got me psyched to go to war.

"I didn't know you knew any Queen songs, Duke," I said.

"There's a time and a place for every piece of music, Earth Angel," he said. "And if you ask me, *this* is the perfect moment for 'We Are the Champions.'"

The skies were overcast when I stepped outside, blanketed with heavy gray clouds. The blue and red lights of local police cruisers flashed at either end of the street, which was otherwise empty of traffic. A chilly wind blew through the silence, carrying the strong smell of mineral-rich water all the way from Smoke Ring Lake.

Briar waved from one of the cruisers, three blocks away, where he'd posted himself after finishing the evacuation. Knowing he was there boosted my spirits, though he had no powers. At least I'd equipped him with special diamond-skinned body armor that would hopefully protect him from whatever the Terralyzers threw at him.

The other three unpowered humans among us also wore the special armor. Roy, who was slung with guns and ammo, jogged over to join Briar. Rusty, also kitted out like a walking arsenal, went the other direction, joining Deputy Jim Withers at the second vehicle.

Ashanti and Phaola staked out positions midway between the office and either end of the street. Mahoney, Minthe, and Nephelae clustered near the office, forming an inner ring of defense.

As for me, I waited in the last place I wanted to be—smack in the middle of our defenses, surrounded by protectors. I'd let them talk me out of going straight to the front line, where I could be of the most use—though I wouldn't stay back for long if the fight got ugly.

And if worse came to worst, and I had to fall back on my secret plan, I'd be on a front line all my own.

"When will they get here, I wonder?" asked Luna, who waited at my side, a last defense. If the enemy punched through this far, and my powers went on the fritz again, she'd try to fend off the attackers. She could also wake Blue Knob Mountain and Prince Gallitzin State Park, whom we'd carried from the back room to the front door area. We'd keep the two of them in reserve, since Veritas had said we should hesitate before waking them.

"Soon, I hope." I nodded and zipped up my leather jacket against the wind. "I'd like to get this over with and get back to planning exotic tours for demigods and nymphs seeking eco-friendly adventure."

Just then, Duke emerged from the office, carrying a paper go-cup filled with steaming brew. "Last call for coffee," he said, handing it over. "At least until you're done kicking behind like the magnificent specimen you are."

"Thanks, Duke." Gratefully, I inhaled the aroma from the pour spout on the black plastic lid, then had a sip.

"Everybody ready?" Duke rolled up his sleeves.

"As we'll ever be," I told him between sips. "Considering we don't know exactly who or what will show up."

"A 'small army,'" said Luna. "Whatever that means."

"I assure you both, it's nothing we can't handle," said Duke. "Do not be intimidated by suggestions to the contrary."

"No matter what happens, sis," said Luna, "I want you to know I love you. I'm sorry we were so distant for so long, but I'm glad we're here together now."

Suddenly, a gunshot rang out from up the street, and the moment of sisterly bonding was broken. We all looked in the direction of the shot, toward Briar's cruiser.

Just as we did so, the cruiser came flying past in midair, upside-down.

"Time's up," said Duke.

The second cruiser shot up the street from the other direction, on its side, and collided with the first in a shattering crash just half a block away.

Even as the smashed hulks of the cars dropped to the pavement in a heap of twisted metal with horns blaring, we edged out into the street for a better look at the action. Up the street, Briar and Roy fired round after round at a trio of floating attackers—even as bursts of brilliant white light flashed toward them from the attackers' upraised hands. Thankfully, the bursts of light were deflected by the armor I'd provided, enabling Briar and Roy to stay on their feet and keep shooting.

Down the street, a second trio of airborne invaders took fire from Deputy Withers and Rusty, seemingly without suffering a single impact. Then, as I watched, the woman at the head of the group of attackers shot a bolt of golden flame downward, and the ground shook violently, toppling both Withers and Rusty.

Ashanti launched herself into the air and flew to help them, even as Phaola soared toward Briar and Roy. That left the middle of the street, the stretch in front of the office, wide open.

But it didn't stay that way for long. Seconds after it cleared, that patch of the street rumbled and buckled, then heaved upward and blew apart in a cloud of dust and debris.

When the cloud cleared, I saw a single figure rising from the crater—a beautiful woman with brown hair streaming in all directions, haloed in pulsing red light.

She was followed by a second figure—a bronze-skinned man encircled by swirls of glittering sand—and a third—a blue-skinned woman born aloft by a muddy waterspout.

The three of them hung there a moment, their glowing eyes locked on me as if taking my measure. For my part, I already knew who they were—who their bodies had belonged to before Terralyze had possessed them, that is.

"I know them all," I told Luna and Duke. "The one in the middle is the Washington state volcano, Mount St. Helens. The man with the sand is the Mojave Desert. And the woman in the water is the Mississippi River."

"So they sent us the third string?" said Luna. "And here I was hoping for a *challenge.*"

"Just remember who the *boss* is," said Duke as he dug into his pockets (and through his earthen substance) for something he could use. "You are *Mother Earth,* and *they* are just *babies* compared to you."

"Babies under the control of novice *assholes*," said Luna. "Let's teach 'em a lesson, big sis."

I stood for a long moment, staring at the figures who had risen from the hole in the street. I reached out with my mind, feeling for the power seething within the planet, ready to bend it to my will— and felt nothing.

Panic whirled within me. If my link to the Earth was broken again, I'd be powerless before those heavy hitters' assault.

Heart hammering, I tried again, reaching desperately for some trace of the connection that would let me tap my greatest source of strength.

This time, the connection blazed to life, and my body filled with the burning energy of an entire planet leaping to obey my commands.

I made it a point to strike first. Crouching, I touched the pavement and funneled my power into it, directing a quake at the three Terralyzers. I followed it fast with a shot of pure force that blew open a fissure from one side of the street to the other.

The fissure split the crater down the middle, dropping Mojave out of sight. Mount St. Helens and Mississippi were already aloft, though, and stayed that way.

I followed the quake with a bombardment of rocks launched out of the fissure, leaping toward Mount St. Helens and Mississippi. Some made contact, pelting the women's heads and upper bodies, but others were deflected by streams of lava from Mount St. Helens' hands or jets of water from Mississippi's.

Mississippi turned the jets on me next, catching me by surprise and shoving me backward. Luckily, I had a friend who could turn Mississippi's watery jets back against her with powers of his own.

Mahoney, who had the power of the mighty Youghiogheny River behind him, twisted Mississippi's jets around so they blasted her right in the face. She screamed and flopped over into the wave surging behind her, disappearing into the muddy foam.

I quickly recovered from the impact of her attack, raising my arms to channel a blast of my own—but before I could let it go, Mount St. Helens threw both hands forward, unleashing a fireball of sizzling lava right at me.

Mahoney raised a wall of water in its path, but the fireball seared through it in a cloud of steam. Digging through the pavement with my powers, I reached for a slab of granite under the street and tried bringing it up fast and hard—but my link to the rock flickered, and it wouldn't budge.

At the last second, though, the fireball dropped suddenly to the street as if it weighed at least a ton.

Looking left, I saw Luna shoot me a quick nod, indicating she'd taken out the ball of lava with her power to manipulate weight and mass.

Unfortunately, we didn't have time for a thank-you. More fireballs were racing toward us, plus raging dust devils spun out of the hands of Mojave, who'd reappeared from his fall in the crater.

Concentrating hard, I made contact with the sand in the whirlwinds, striving to seize control. The sand resisted at first, then gave in, peeling away from the central force that propelled it. Instead of whipping the hell out of me and Luna, it curled back and swirled around Mojave's head, peppering him with grit and jumping in his eyes.

As for the fireballs, Luna dropped them as fast as they launched with crackling weight-control beams. They hissed when they hit, burning down through the pavement like acid through paper.

"Fighting back is hopeless!" shouted Mount St. Helens. "We're *trained* for combat! Sooner or later, we'll take you down!"

None of us wasted our breath talking back. I reached for the granite slab again, nearly freeing it, as Luna threw her weight control at St. Helen's, forcing her to hunch. Mahoney wheeled his arms in the air, shredding Mississippi's wave and exposing the blue-skinned woman snarling inside.

Even the nymphs took a stab at the pile-on. Nephelae conjured up a cloud of mist, seasoned with one of Minthe's potent herbal powders, and sent it gliding toward Mount St. Helen's. The cloud wafted right in her face, then suddenly thickened, forming a solid green block over her features.

We had them on the ropes. Next, we had to knock them out and help our friends elsewhere on the street.

"Make them sleep," I told Luna. "Put them under."

Luna looked like she was straining. "Working on it, sis! There's some kind of *interference*."

Just as she said it, a blast of flame roared down from above, barely missing us. Before I could get my bearings, another blast swept down from a different spot in the sky, and then another from somewhere else.

Looking up as we scattered, I saw the source, just as I had that day out at Smoke Ring Lake. Three masses of dark cloud broke free from the blanket above us, glowing orange at one end with the promise of searing flame banked and ready to blast from within.

The Terralyzers were pulling out all the stops. They'd brought along fire-breathing drones just in case the mind-controlled Landkind weren't enough to overwhelm us.

One bolt of blistering flame after another lanced down from the cloud-drones, barely missing us as we ran for cover.

My Highlander wasn't as lucky as we were. It got torched when Luna, Duke, and I sheltered behind it, set ablaze from three different drones in three different directions.

Furious, I reached for a slab of cement sidewalk with my power, wrenching it up out of the ground and hurling it at the nearest drone. The slab spun up and caught the drone square across the flamethrowing end, smashing it to bits.

As the pieces of the shattered drone pelted down, Luna charged out from behind the flaming Highlander with arms held high. Beams of light slashed up from her fingertips and struck a second drone; it wobbled as she boosted its weight, working to drag it down.

Then, a spear of hardened sand from Mojave punched into her gut, sending her reeling. Mojave and his partners were back in the game.

The weight-shifting ended as Luna took the blow, and the cloud-shrouded drone turned its fiery maw in her direction. The maw glowed brighter, about to fire...

And a jet of water from Mahoney's hands stabbed into it, extinguishing the flame before it could spew out at us.

Duke and I ran to help Luna, even as Mount St. Helens burned the green mass off her face with superheated fingertips. With a bellow of rage, she rose higher and glowed brighter, pulsing red and gold.

Everyone and everything we faced opened fire on us at the same time. St. Helens let loose with a volley of fireballs, and Mojave fired fused-sand blades. Mississippi churned out a high-velocity water-spout, and the two remaining drones rained down rivers of fire.

With a desperate act of will, I managed to dredge up a huge sheet of granite from underground and drape it over most of us just in time. Minthe, Nephelae, Duke, Luna, and I huddled under that curtain of stone as the flame, fireballs, blades, and waterspout splashed over it in a punishing wave.

Peering around the edge of the shield, I saw Mahoney was still taking a pounding on his own, holding back the worst of the onslaught—just barely—with a barrier of river rock he'd erected.

More tongues of fire lashed down from the drones, and more balls of flaming lava smashed into my granite shield. If the barrage continued for much longer, I wasn't sure we could hold out against it, let alone win the fight.

As if to reinforce my thinking, my control of the shield slipped, and it slumped toward us. Gritting my teeth, I clawed for my link to the Earth, hooking it like a fish trying to wriggle away. Fresh energy sizzled through the connection, and I channeled it into the shield, shoring it up just in time for another assault.

When that latest bombardment ceased, I popped up from behind the granite for a look at the full extent of the battlefield. Glancing up the street, I saw Phaola trading energy blasts with two male Terralyzers, even as Briar and Roy, in their diamond armor, fired guns at a third who had them pinned down behind a truck. Down the street, I saw Ashanti struggling hand-to-hand with another Terralyzer lit by a flaring nimbus of golden energy. Even as they tumbled through the sky, Deputy Withers and Rusty fired rifles at two other energized enemies marching inexorably toward them.

My gut churned as I ducked back down behind the barrier, just missing a strike by an incoming salvo of deadly force. Everyone was fully engaged, and our side wasn't winning. It was then I realized the time had come for the strategy I'd been keeping to myself.

"Luna!" I grabbed her by the shoulder. "You're in charge! Whatever you do, hold the line!"

"Why?" She looked confused. "Where are *you* going?"

"I have to step away," I said. "Hopefully not for long."

"We need you *here*," said Duke. "We need all hands on deck!"

"You'll have to manage without me." Even as I said it, I was getting ready to leave, feeling around underfoot for the ley line network that ran through the skin of the Earth. "I know you can do it."

"Earth Angel, no!" shouted Duke.

But I was already gone before he could say another word, my body slumping to the pavement as my mind dove into the ley lines of crackling geologic energy.

The ley line network was as old as the world itself, and I knew it well. I could use it to travel from place to place, investigate trouble spots, repair damage...and, in this case, track the forces of darkness to their source.

Diving into the system, I spotted signs of the Terralyzers right away—roiling balls of disruption among the shimmering tendrils threaded through my town. Wasting no time, I zipped toward the closest one and threw myself into orbit around it like a planet around a blazing sun.

I could have done some damage from there, but that wasn't my goal. Instead, I continued to circle, feeling around for the one thing I'd deserted my body to find.

And there it was. A single slender strand of incandescent white light ran from the belly of the pulsating yellow sphere and shot off through the glowing web of the network.

As soon as I saw that white strand, I knew it was exactly what I wanted—a trail to follow. I shot over and raced along it as fast as I could go, skimming the radiant beam like a surfer riding a wave.

As I went, I saw other strands of the same size and whiteness, branches leading to other Terralyzers in the conflict. I flew past them, staying fixed on the branch I was riding.

They all led to the same main conduit, though—a thicker, brighter strand from which they all got their power. I rode my own branch to the intersection point and shunted onto it, then took off like a bullet from a gun, propelled by the conduit's higher energy.

I picked up speed the further I got from the battle, rocketing through the glowing network. The sparks of other minds and phenomena flared around me, riding other lines and leaping between them.

At first, I had a vague sense of where I might be, what topography sprawled above—but it faded as my speed picked up. Soon, I lost all track of where I was or how far I'd gone; it could as easily have been ten miles from home as a thousand, five minutes away as fifty hours.

It's possible to get lost inside yourself, especially when you're a planet. Down in the darkness among the glowing strands, everything looks the same. You start to wonder if you'll ever find your way out.

After a while, though, the darkness brightened, and the conduit heated and swelled. I had the feeling it was taking me somewhere important—not home, but somewhere I badly needed to be.

Then, suddenly, the conduit carried me up to a dazzling white orb that was spinning fast within a gleaming crimson shell. It was there that the conduit ended, piercing the side of the orb so it flared with blinding white light. I could feel the energy racing up the line and into the orb, burning hot as it entered the furnace.

Scrambling off the line before I got cooked, I found myself afloat, drifting around the pulsating orb. It wasn't until it spoke to me, however, that I knew for sure I'd come to the right place—the source of the power controlling Landkind.

Thank you for coming. The orb's voice sounded male and deep. *By leaving your body, you have saved me the trouble of hollowing you out.*

A wave of panic shot through me. I'd expected to be the one doing the surprising.

It never occurred to me until *just then* that my own plan had led me into a *trap.*

That's right, said the mind inside the orb. *I wanted you here for my own purposes. My own satisfaction. That has always been my only goal.*

Focusing my thoughts, I beamed them across the space around the orb. *I thought your goal was to serve the United States military. To put the soul of the world under their control.*

I was buffeted by rippling waves of energy as the orb laughed. They *have been serving* me*! And I serve only* myself*!*

Confused, I struggled to understand. *Who are you? What are you talking about?*

Don't you remember me? Again, the orb laughed. *Well, you should. You and I go* waaay *back.*

How far back? I asked.

Sixty-six million years back! roared the orb. *Does that ring any bells?*

I dug deep into my memory, tunneling back as far as I could—and found myself wishing I'd spent more time studying my own history. Beyond a certain point, the past became a blur, a muddle of sensory input mashed together.

I don't know, I said. *I don't remember.*

You have to! snapped the orb. *It was the biggest and most destructive event in your history! It was the thing that hurt you more than anything before or since!*

I still don't know, I said.

With a cry of enraged frustration, he beamed a stream of images and sensations into my mind. It was too much for me at first, and I recoiled—but then, with a monumental effort, I dug in and stood my ground.

The download washed over me with agonizing vividness—the massive rock plunging from the sky, crashing into the Earth with devastating force. Solid rock rippling like water from the impact, shooting walls of fiery pellets like hails of bullets in all directions. Firestorms surging out in rings from the impact zone, cooking every living thing instantaneously. The shrieks of the dying drowned out by the roar of the storms and aftershocks, the thunderous crash of waves massive enough to flood entire continents.

The screams of the world itself as it wobbled in its orbit, rocked to the core by the pulverizing blow. *My* screams, resounding across millions of years with the pain and terror of a planet torn asunder.

Hearing them echo in my mind, it all came back to me. I *remembered*...and immediately wished I had not.

The asteroid! said the orb. *The one that made the Gulf of Mexico and wiped out nearly every living thing! I am that asteroid's life force, dredged up from the Chixculub crater by offshore drillers, reawakened to finish my mission after all these millions of years.*

What mission is that? I asked.

Complete takeover of your world from the inside out, said the orb. *Annihilation of all lifeforms and replacement with those grown from the seeds I brought with me from my distant launch point. I will remake your world,* said the orb, *and you can't do a thing to stop me!*

You had a mission? Even among the myriad of memories I'd retrieved, this jumped out at me. It was a complete surprise, something I'd never considered in 66 million years.

It cast the long-ago disaster of Chixculub in a terrible new light. If that asteroid collision in ancient times was intentional, not an accident, then the whole thing had been an *attack*. An *invasion*.

And according to the orb, the threat was not only real, it was *resurgent*. It had been at the heart of the Terralyze menace all along.

Given that, it didn't take much to piece together other facts, too.

The minds implanted in the hollowed-out Landkind, I said. *They don't belong to human soldiers at all, do they?*

Of course not, said the orb. *Those minds are all pieces of me. Fragments of the* Allself *sent to reshape and rule this world as the paradise it was always meant to be—which to you and yours will seem an endless nightmare.*

But you failed before, I said.

A slight miscalculation in my angle of approach, said the orb, the Allself. *I never meant to hit so hard or bury myself so deep. But my millions of years of waiting and planning were well spent, and I will not fail again.*

Even as he spoke, I drifted around him, picking my moment. One of us had to make the first move, and I thought I'd stand the best chance if it was me.

Still, I knew the risk would be great. Going into battle without knowing the enemy's full capabilities could be a recipe for disaster.

But I'd come here—wherever "here" was—to do a job, and that job was more important than ever. I wasn't just facing off with a government project hoping to install a puppet in the driver's seat of the Earth. I was confronting a truly alien force with the goal of remaking the world in the image of an alien nightmare-scape.

By far, it was the biggest fight of my life...and I had no one to back me up or ease my burden. Every last bit of it was on my shoulders.

And time was running out. He was telling me so.

By the way, your friends are almost beaten, said the Allself. *I see their struggles through the eyes of my shock troops, and they cannot win. They won't last much longer.*

You're wrong. I kept circling him, gathering my strength and will for what was about to happen. *They're tougher than you can imagine.*

Waves of laughter rippled out from the Allself. *You're a funny little planet-soul, you know that? I almost hate to execute you.*

I looped around him again and again, building up steam and courage. I felt so vulnerable in my non-corporeal form, little more than a spark of energy—though, in truth, that spark was just a focal point, and the vast reaches of my full potential lay far beyond the limited space in which I floated.

The thing is, you've been doing a shitty job as a world, said the Allself. *And we both know it. You ought to be relieved that I'm taking the place off your hands.*

It was then that I finally let loose, blasting away with everything I had. Because I knew he was telling the truth, at least a little.

That was why I unleashed such a punishing bombardment of raw energy, channeled directly from my distant, molten core. I shot it right into the heart of the Allself's orb, blitzing its consciousness with seething, scalding power.

Subjected to this barrage of pure force, the orb flared and spun, recoiling from the attack. Where was its sarcasm now? What happened to its predictions of my defeat and execution?

The orb contracted, tightening its circumference under the blistering assault. I kept it up, intensifying the burn with every intention of wiping him out.

Then, suddenly, the orb expanded violently, ejecting a concussive wave that hurled me across the crimson shell. More waves followed, pinning me to the gleaming curve of the shell, hammering me as I stuck there.

Not enough, little pinprick, roared the Allself. *You took your best shot, but it wasn't enough. And now you are depleted and at the mercy of your replacement!*

The pressure of his grip increased. I strained to break free but could not.

That was when I realized he was going to stay true to his promise. He was going to kill and replace me, and there was nothing I could do about it.

*D**ie, little world-gnat! howled the Allself as he pummeled me with one blow after another. Your time has passed! Your people are doomed! Let the void take you and be done with it!*

I felt myself weakening. His power was just too great to resist—too *alien*. Every time I gathered strength and pushed back, he adapted, changing the wavelengths and other properties of his unique energy to scramble my own resistance.

*Surrender now, and I promise not to slaughter your friends...*too *painfully.* He laughed and hammered away with ever-stronger bursts of energy, keeping me on the ropes.

I suddenly realized that I might be about to die. Though I'd come here full of confidence and ferocity, I'd underestimated the enemy. I hadn't expected to find some ancient alien force that had brutalized me in the distant past, some vengeful monster that had spent the past 66 million years planning and powering up to destroy me.

Now there I was, suffering under an onslaught I couldn't deflect, my spark growing dimmer with each fresh blast.

It feels good to finish old business, said the Allself as he lashed out again and again. *To finally put the past behind me. To finally put* you *behind me.*

I cringed as bolts of agony shot through me like blazing hot shrapnel through flesh. I couldn't imagine withstanding this kind of relentless assault for much longer.

The truth is, part of me wanted to surrender and let the Allself destroy me. I'd been careless and selfish, putting off delving into my legacy as Mother Earth in favor of staying in my safe little world with Briar, Duke, and the rest. I'd done some good and saved some lives, but I'd turned my back on most of my responsibilities and hadn't kept watch over my friends the way I should have.

Maybe, if I'd been paying attention and really standing guard, Phaola and the others wouldn't have been victimized. Maybe I could have stopped the Allself's scheme before it got as far as it did.

Maybe now, with the fate of the world teetering into darkness, though I once could have stopped it, I deserved everything I got.

So this is how it feels to murder a world, said the Allself. *This is how it feels to do what I was born to do.*

I got in some shots of my own, knocking him off balance, but only briefly. He came back stronger than ever, jackhammering my consciousness with a flurry of strikes that left me dazed and vulnerable.

I'm almost sorry it's over, he said. *This is by far the most satisfying experience I've ever had.*

Another blow sailed in, and another. The agony intensified to the point of being unbearable.

And then he made it *worse.*

Before you die, here's a little gift to send you off. He laughed, shaping another charge from the churn of his bodiless energy form. *Enjoy this peek at what's happening back home. One last glimpse of your precious loved ones so you'll perish with their suffering faces in your mind.*

He hurled the charge, sending it careening like ball lightning across the gap between us. As soon as it struck me, my mind's eye was flooded with images of Confluence.

Bodies were scattered in the street—some still, some struggling in vain to get up and continue the fight. Every one of them was one of my people—Phaola, Luna, Minthe, Nephelae, Mahoney, Roy, Rusty…Briar. As I watched, Ashanti joined them, hurled to the pavement by blasts of energy from all directions. That left the Terralyzers on their feet and hovering over the battlefield, grinning at the decisive victory they'd achieved.

Only one man stood to oppose them. Duke stepped out from behind the twisted wreckage of a pickup truck, head held high and shoulders squared. He walked toward them, yanking live grenades from the earthen matter of his belly. He pulled the pins with his teeth and wound his arms back to pitch, even as the drones and vicious enforcers converged around him, ready to pounce.

It was the moment before his death—his *second* death—and I knew it. That was when the view of Confluence winked out. My mind's eye was cut off from the scene.

Don't worry, said the Allself. *You'll all be together again very soon, reunited in death. You see? I'm doing you a favor.*

I seethed against the smooth crimson curve of the shell, remembering every detail of the vision he'd shown me. The sight of my friends' defeat and impending annihilation was burned forever into my mind, spawning storms of rage and hatred swirling within me.

Just remember, as you cease to exist, said the Allself. *You have yourself to thank for what's happened to your friends. Their deaths are on your head.*

Every word was like a bullet to my heart. Every bit of me wanted to scream in pain at once.

Now close your eyes, pitiful planet, said the Allself. *This could get messy.*

The orb spun and crackled, building up a charge. Tongues of fire lashed and arced across his surface in rhythmic leaps, as if they were chasing each other.

Then the Allself rolled toward me, and I knew he was hell-bent on my eradication.

I just waited there, watching him advance, feeling his heat getting closer—thinking about Duke and all the others. It was just as well I died now, rather than live to go home and see what was left of them. It was better not to have to see their accusing faces glaring up at me in death.

But what if there was still a way to save them? What if I could still open the floodgates of my power, though I'd spent so much time keeping them closed?

The words of Veritas, Goddess of Truth, returned to me: *All the power of all the world is at your fingertips, everywhere, always.*

If *she* said it, it had to be *true,* didn't it? It had to mean I could do much more than I *thought* I could.

I remembered my battered friends again, on the brink of extinction, and I thought of something else Veritas had said: *Open yourself to the possibilities, and you will be* unstoppable.

As I thought of all that, something started to change within me. My fear and shame and guilt scuttled away like cockroaches in the light of day. My anger expanded and unfolded, filling me from edge to edge—and then the edges fell away. Everything holding me back fell away all at once.

Suddenly, I felt power all around, gushing into me without my having to reach for it. *Waterfalls* of power poured in from everywhere, inundating me, filling me with more energy than I'd ever contained before, at least all at once. It was almost too much to handle, too much to withstand—so much power, it might have *destroyed* me had I been any weaker.

But Mother Earth could handle all that and more. *Bring it on*, I said, gulping it greedily, feeling it surge and boil within me.

Die! roared the Allself as he launched his latest and greatest charge at me. *Let the new age begin!*

But when the blast finally hit me, it splashed off harmlessly. The power I'd been soaking up dwarfed that of the Allself, deflecting his biggest strike yet without the slightest strain.

What?! The Allself sounded shocked. *But that isn't* possible!

I didn't say a word to him. I had other work to occupy my time, like preparing to give him some much-deserved payback.

You should be dead now! howled the Allself. *You should have been extinguished!*

Silently, I stirred the flames banking within me. All the vast cataracts of power flooding into me fueled the fire, building it into a superheated blaze like the nuclear heart of the sun.

It doesn't matter! The Allself cooked up another blast of his own, hypercharged energy pulled from his blistering core. *This time, you will die! The Earth will be* my *world for the rest of eternity!*

No sooner had those words left him than I unleashed the massive torrent of power I'd been channeling. He screamed as it rushed over him, a firestorm of energy drawn from every corner of the planet.

His pain only made me want to keep the punishment coming. I didn't let up the slightest bit; if anything, I opened the channel wider, letting through more power with each passing second. It came from everywhere—hurricane winds, the rays of the sun, the tides of the ocean, the grinding of the continental plates. It barreled through the ley line network, merging into a single beam of overwhelming force that punched through the Allself's once-formidable presence as if it were tissue paper.

And even as this incredible power poured through me, I felt every mile of its journey, every moment of its existence. I sensed its role in the systems of the world, its connection to the enormous complexity of the Earth. My awareness flared far beyond the Allself's base, sweeping out around the globe in all directions at once—restoring my grasp of the vast and elaborate planet I'd been born to represent and defend.

I'd forgotten just how massive and miraculous it was. I'd shied away from experiencing its immensity, from using its gargantuan power as I saw fit.

But not anymore.

I held nothing back as I blasted away at the Allself. Roaring with rage and horror, he blew apart under the assault, the coalesced energy of his consciousness shredding irreversibly. I didn't stop, however, until every last shred of his mind was burned away as if it had never existed.

Then, without wasting a single second, I dove into the ley lines and rocketed toward Confluence, traveling faster than I ever had through the network that girdled my crust.

Breaking out of the network in Confluence, I burst back into my human body, which I quickly realized was still alive. As soon as my energy flowed back into that form, my eyes shot open. I saw the granite shield above me, the one I'd whipped up for cover before leaving.

Sitting up, I worked to get my bearings and adjust to the reconnection of spirit and flesh. I knew it hadn't been ages since I'd been whole, but it felt like it.

I also hoped it hadn't been as long as it seemed since the Allself had shown me my friends on the verge of annihilation. I hoped there was still a chance I could save them.

Jumping to my feet, I stepped out from behind the shield and gazed at the street, dreading what I might see. Thankfully, I'd arrived soon after the moment the Allself had shown me. Duke had just thrown a grenade at the converging Terralyzers and was about to pitch another. The first exploded as the enemy scattered, knocking down Mojave and Mississippi but not doing any damage to the rest.

While he distracted them, I crouched and touched the street, triggering a chain reaction of fast-moving fissures. They neatly avoided Duke and zipped straight for the Terralyzers on the ground, opening wide just in time to swallow up three of them, including Mojave. They screamed all the way to the bowels of the Earth.

Duke glanced over his shoulder at me and smiled, then let the second grenade fly. The Terralyzers moved away from it easily, staying out of its path—at least until I got involved.

With a wave of my arm, I summoned a shower of dirt from the ground nearby and cast it up, sending it in an arc toward the grenade. The dirt collided with the grenade, shunting it off on a new route perpendicular to its original arc.

A route that flung it at two male Terralyzers before they could get away. It exploded between them, blasting their bodies far apart onto piles of rubble, leaving them smoking, blood-soaked wrecks.

Enraged, Mount St. Helens wheeled around, hands pointing at Duke and flaring with energy ready to be released. Her expression turned into total shock, however, when she caught sight of me behind her target.

"*Gaia?*" Her hands flared brighter, building a charge. "But the Allself *trapped* you. You were *doomed.*"

"Wrong." I summoned rocks the size of watermelons from inside the widest fissures and sent them hurtling at her from six different directions at once. "The *Allself* was doomed. And now, so are *you.*"

A pair of airborne drones zapped two of the big rocks with their flamethrowers, knocking them away. Mount St. Helens hurled aside another two with her lava fireballs, sending them tumbling over the battlefield.

But two of them still got through. One crashed into her back, pitching her forward, while the other drove her back with a heavy blow to the chest. Crying out, Mount St. Helens toppled to the street in a tangle of limbs and rocks, laid low.

From there, I went through the others like a scythe through wheat, cranking out one rapid-fire attack after another. No intermittent power loss lessened my might or gave the enemy a chance to gain ground. I unleashed a series of rock bombardments, earthquakes, sinkholes, and mud bursts one after another, battering and immobilizing my opponents in quick succession.

I was fighting like a planet *ought* to fight, putting all my weapons to work at once, taking no prisoners. Giving no quarter to the bastards who'd shown my own people no mercy. Coming down like a real Mother Earth, not just a private detective with some stone-throwing skills.

The Terralyzers went down hard, bashed into submission. Next, I turned my attention skyward, hoisting chunks of rock and taking aim at the two drones circling above me.

Just as I was getting ready to fire the granite at them, I heard a loud *crack*. I felt a hard impact in my left shoulder that spun me around and hurt like hell.

Gunshot. It didn't take a genius to figure that out...though the source of the shot turned out to be a surprise.

Quickly looking in the direction from which the bullet had come, I saw a familiar man and woman standing behind my own granite shield—Agent Frank Wagner and Agent Judy Lewis of the F.B.I. Frank held a rifle, Judy a pistol, and both barrels were pointed dead-on at me.

"You really skunked our operation here, didn't you?" shouted Frank. "Top to freakin' bottom."

"Good thing we've got a five-star *backup plan*," hollered Judy as she cranked off one shot after another, pumping a hail of bullets in my direction.

Once upon a time, catching a slug in the shoulder might have slowed me down a little. The shock from such a gunshot wound might have put me off my game.

But this was by no means that kind of time. I'd just defeated an ancient and powerful threat from beyond the stars, saving the world from alien domination. I was at the peak of my powers and loaded for bear.

Getting tagged by an F.B.I. ambush in the heat of battle was one thing, but getting perforated by a follow-up shower of lead that I saw coming was quite another.

Even as Judy's bullets raced toward me, I deflected them with a spray of gravel—each bullet winged by one perfectly propelled gravel nugget. Not a single shot made it through that field of rico-chets; every bullet went zinging into smoldering debris or jagged fissures...or the ground at Frank and Judy's feet, barely missing the tips of their shoes.

With that first volley disposed of, I made my next move. Spreading my arms wide, I summoned tons of rock and dirt from under the pavement, heaving it up into a massive, towering figure. As I wove my hands through the air, the matrix of earthen matter whirled and flowed, taking on the contours of a giant human form.

My human form.

The two drones swooped toward Giant Gaia with flamethrowers

belching out tongues of fire. By then, I'd hardened the giant's body, giving it the approximate strength of solid diamond. When Giant Gaia with her ultra-tough hide smacked one drone and then the other, they both hurtled into nearby buildings at high speed and blew apart.

More bullets raced toward me, and I flipped them away with bits of gravel. Meanwhile, Giant Gaia turned her full attention on Frank and Judy, and I saw them through her eyes as they filled up with terror.

Swinging their guns up, they fired everything they had at Giant Gaia, peppering her with bullets—but every shot bounced off her hardened shell. Nothing they had could put a dent in her.

But *she* had no such problem with *them.* Letting loose a roar of rage, she scooped up Judy and shook her until she dropped her weapon. That was when Frank stopped shooting and ran, sprinting through the body-littered battleground.

But he came up short in his flight when one of the bodies suddenly rose up to confront him. It was Ashanti, face bloodied but otherwise looking serenely transfigured, utterly wise and goddess-like.

"I got my memory back," she said, her voice echoing. "Did you know that, Agent Wagner? When the Earth Mother reconnected with her fullest power and destroyed the Allself, a *lot* of things were corrected."

Teeth clenched, Frank whipped his rifle around and cranked off shot after shot. Every shell that left his weapon melted like wax, and then the weapon melted, too. He flung it aside with a cry of pain.

"I remember you were part of the Hollowing team," said Ashanti. "And you *enjoyed* your work, didn't you? Wiping out the souls of Landkind wasn't a guilt trip for you *at all*, was it?"

Frank spun and tried to run, but Ashanti flicked him off his feet with a blast of golden energy. Then she glided inexorably toward him, the pulse of her blazing aura growing stronger with each passing second.

"You should have *known* better, Frank," said Ashanti. "You can't get *away* with that kind of shit anymore."

Frank was in a complete panic, scrambling in the rubble. His confidence was shattered, his self-control destroyed. He knew all too well what outcome his future likely held.

"The Earth and its wonders have been screwed over long enough," said Ashanti. "Consider this your *me too moment,* you asshole."

Then, as Frank desperately clambered to his feet, she unleashed a beam of blistering energy that engulfed him in its brilliance. Frank screamed his lungs out as the power of the Grand Canyon itself vaporized him, turning every molecule in his body into wispy steam.

"Good riddance." Ashanti turned slowly, scanning the street with her brightly-glowing eyes. "Now who's next?"

"Nobody." I approached her, leaving Giant Gaia with Judy still firmly in her grip. "It's finally over."

Ashanti sniffed, looking more regal than ever. "I don't see why we can't butcher every last one of them."

"Because they weren't acting of their own free will," I told her, gesturing at two of the unconscious, possessed Landkind on the pavement nearby. "And we need to see if we can change them back to the way they used to be."

"I suppose you're right," said Ashanti. "After all, *I* was able to return to my old self."

To someone like me, who'd known her only during her time of memory loss, that wasn't quite right. The Ashanti with amnesia *was* her "old self" as far as I was concerned.

But getting to know the new, true Ashanti would have to wait. Someone else's welfare was foremost in my mind and required immediate attention.

I didn't know if Briar was even alive.

Turning from Ashanti, I hurried up the street, looking all around as I went. Amid the smoking rubble, I saw Terralyzers sprawled alongside my people, all of them cut, bruised, bloody, and out cold.

Mahoney lay under chunks of pavement, silent and still. Further along, Luna was huddled behind the severed backend of a police cruiser, her face and arms battered and singed.

Then, I saw diamond-skinned body armor half a block away and broke into a run. The man inside it lay spread-eagled, facing away from me atop a high pile of shattered cinderblock, a mangled spear of rebar jutting from his belly.

Heart slamming in my chest, I raced to that figure, dreading what I would find. Was this the sacrifice I'd made to stop the Terralyzers? Had I given up the man I loved when I raced off through the ley line network to destroy the Allself?

Breathless, I clawed my way up the pile. Tears welled up as I reached the man in the armor and touched his hand, which was heavy and cold.

No no no no no no no

Then I heard *his* voice call out to me from not far away. "Gaia...help me..."

And intense relief flooded into my hammering heart.

Turning the head of the man on the pile, I saw he was Deputy Withers, not Briar.

"Gaia...please..."

Following Briar's voice, I saw he was half-buried under a mound of debris. Hurrying to his side, I flung away the debris with a wave of my hand, freeing him.

"My leg's broken." He sounded weak and in pain, and he was having trouble breathing...but at least the armor had kept him alive and minimized his injuries. "I think...I busted some ribs, too."

I heard familiar sirens in the distance. Emergency vehicles were on their way. "I'm just glad you're alive," I whispered in his ear. "You're going to be okay."

Then, gently, I leaned down and kissed his face. My soul overflowed with joy at the touch of his skin, the feel of his breath, the smell of his cheek. In spite of everything, we had another chance at life and love, a new beginning from the ashes and blood. This, right here, was happiness.

I, for one, wasn't going to throw it away.

EPILOGUE

S *ix weeks later...*
    "It's time," said Duke. "Go ahead and start."

"Will do." Luna sat at her desk with a laptop in front of her, waiting to activate the link to the online teleconference. Thanks to a new digital projector, everyone in the office could see the teleconference interface beamed onto the whiteboard on the wall.

We all watched as Luna hit the button, and the teleconference screen appeared. Small windows showing people from various locations were stacked on the right side of the screen. A large window dominated the left side, displaying the moderator of the meeting.

In this case, that was the Grand Canyon herself, Ashanti Moneta. She was broadcasting live from her home in Arizona, where she'd returned soon after the battle.

"Welcome," she said, "to the first session of the Council of Landkind."

Sitting on the edge of Luna's desk, I nodded and smiled. The Council was something new and overdue, formed in the aftermath of the Terralyzer conflict. Six weeks after Landkind and I had nearly been conquered by hostile forces, we had a formal troubleshooting and decision-making body to help avert such crises in the future...and Ashanti was its President. Clearly, the old way of keeping in touch informally over the ley line network had not been enough to give us the unity and responsiveness we needed.

"Let's begin with some moments of silence to remember those we lost in the war." Ashanti bowed her head. "Mahoney Wells was one of the best of us. Ohiopyle and the Youghiogheny River will never be the same."

"To Mahoney." We all said it at once, then fell silent—including Roy Price, Mahoney's appointed successor, whom I could see in one of the windows on the screen. As always, he was shoulder to shoulder with Rusty.

After a moment, Ashanti spoke again. "Minthe, a nymph of the secret garden and devoted friend of Landkind to the end. No one shall tend the herbs of the Earth so well as she."

"To Minthe." We all said it except Nephelae, who sat despondent in a corner of the room. The rest of us had lost a great friend and source of light and joy; Nephelae, however, had lost the partner of a lifetime.

A moment of silence passed, and Ashanti again spoke. "Deputy Jim Withers was not Landkind, but he fought alongside us to preserve our way of life and defend the Earth. Henceforth, we shall remember him as one of our own."

"To Jim Withers," Briar said loudly, and the rest of us followed.

There was another moment of silence before the next remembrance. "Mount St. Helens died under the influence of dark forces, as did Mojave, Salt Lake, and Big Sur. Let there be no mistake: they died as victims and heroes. Their lives of remarkable service must never be forgotten. Their sacrifice will forever be a monument to the fortitude of our kind."

"Mount St. Helens," we said. "Mojave. Salt Lake. Big Sur."

Deep regret washed over me as I thought of those possessed Landkind who'd died in the battle...though I knew their minds and spirits had been burned out long before that. Veritas had helped others reintegrate their personas with their physical bodies—Phaola, Blue Knob Mountain, and Prince Gallitzin State Park, to name a few—but the ones who'd gone down fighting had been lost causes.

Others were lost causes, as well. The Allself was gone, but some of those whom he'd controlled were still broken. "Let us observe a final moment of silence," said Ashanti, "in honor of our fellow Landkind who remain damaged by the Allself's influence. They will never be forsaken."

Everyone fell silent again, considering those poor unfortunate souls. We'd created a place for them, safe and remote, where they could do no further harm. Their powers and realms were transferred to others, their contact with the outside world severed...but at least they could live in peace.

Though peace, for them, would not be the same as freedom.

"All right then," said Ashanti. "We have remembered and honored those who deserve it. Let us now begin in earnest this first session of the Council of Landkind. First order of business?"

"Madame President." Rune Carson, wearing a businesslike black blouse and skirt, walked to the middle of the floor. After all the help she'd provided in infiltrating the ultra-fracking site near Shawnee State Park, she'd been chosen unanimously by the Council to serve as special Humanity-Landkind liaison. "I'd like to propose a new program for reclaiming polluted sites using ley line manipulation and geomantic magic."

"Interesting, Ms. Carson." Ashanti leaned forward on the screen. "Tell us more."

A lopsided grin appeared on Rune's face. "Don't mind if I do."

Later, when the meeting had ended, I refilled my cup of coffee, pulled on my leather jacket, and stepped outside for a breath of fresh air.

"Earth Angel." Duke, as usual, was not far behind me. "Are you all right?"

As we stood in front of the office, I gazed at the street where the battle had taken place. Six weeks after that fight, it had been mostly repaired...but the memory of the smoking, corpse-strewn ruins would never leave me.

"It's almost like it never happened," I said. "Almost."

"*We* remember," said Duke. "We know the truth, even if it's a secret to most of the rest of the world."

I knew he was right, and keeping the truth about Landkind a secret from humanity at large was important, but it still bothered me. After the defeat of the Allself and Terralyzers, a small army of National Guardsmen and federal agents had swept into town—a cleanup detail set on scrubbing all proof of the government's misled and failed project. Without any kind of apology, they'd given us a cover story, and we'd taken it. How else could we avoid the inevitable difficult questions and unwanted attention? How else could we make people believe we weren't crazy or full of shit?

So what if most of humanity would never know of the sacrifices made to beat back the ancient alien invader?

"It still doesn't seem fair," I said. "Mahoney, Minthe, and Withers are all gone, and the world thinks it's because of a gas line explosion."

Duke shrugged. "We both know it was the best route to take, Earth Angel. Telling the truth would have exposed Landkind—and *you.* Not to mention, hardly anyone would have believed it anyway."

And if they had, they might have come to town looking for ways to harness the alien might of the Allself. "I know you're right," I told him. "I just wish there could be...*more* for them."

"The Council memorialized them," said Duke. "That might be the best we can hope for right now."

I knew he was right, though I didn't want to hear it. I kept thinking, as the human avatar of an entire planet, there had to be *something* I could do to make things right...make it all *feel* better. But short of bringing my friends back to life, what else was there to do?

Downtown Confluence had been rebuilt, better than before, with federal money. Cars rolled up and down Casselman Street in the mid-morning sunlight, and shoppers strolled happily from storefront to storefront. The first meeting of the Council of Landkind was in session, promising a brighter future for us all. At a glance, it sure seemed like things were on an upswing.

Why then was "sinking fast" my mood of the day? Why couldn't I just embrace the positivity and get on with my life? Enough with the bipolar shit!

Duke cleared his throat then, breaking my train of thought. "I'm thinking of taking a vacation, Earth Angel. Would that be all right with you?"

I was surprised. It was something he'd never talked about with me. "I suppose. As long as you're not planning a world tour with the Strayhorns."

He looked offended. "My big band? You made it clear: no postmortem world tours." He continued quickly, getting in one more sentence under his breath. "Unless I'm in *disguise*, perhaps."

I smiled. "I'm telling you, Duke, the world isn't ready for a resurrected golem bandleader."

"What about you? Have *you* ever considered taking a vacation?" asked Duke, quickly changing the subject. "Just taking a little time off to go somewhere and see the sights? Or would that be boring for Mother Earth, like looking in a mirror?"

I frowned. "I don't know. I don't have time."

"Nobody does. You have to *make* time."

"But something always comes up," I told him. "It's just one thing after another."

"Life doesn't *have* to be that way," said Duke. "There isn't *always* a nightmare scenario lurking around the corner."

"I feel like it wouldn't be right. I've ducked my responsibilities enough." I shook my head. "Anyway, the *world* isn't *supposed* to take a vacation, is it?"

"Who says so?" Duke shrugged. "Maybe you should give it a try. You *do* run a *travel agency*, after all. It's not as if setting up a *trip* would be a problem."

"Maybe you're right," I said, fiddling with my braid. "Maybe a getaway *would* do me some good. But after all that's happened, I *really* need to get more serious about my role as Earth's avatar."

"Is there a reason you can't do both?" asked Duke. "You could make it a *fact-finding* trip. Or a *royal tour.*"

I wanted to shoot down the idea...but I realized he might be on to something. Maybe some time away was *exactly* what I needed to get more in touch with my inner Mother Earth.

Before I could tell him so, however, the front door of Cruel World Travel/Charmer Investigations flew open, the chime playing "Caravan" as always. Briar ran out, eyes glued to his phone, looking grim and intense.

"Dale, what is it?" I asked, instantly worried.

He read more text on the screen of his phone, scrolling through it with flicks of his thumb. His expression turned grimmer, and his jaws clenched and twitched.

"We need to go, Gaia." His voice was tight with tension. "There's been another murder."

"Who?" My heart hammered in my chest like a trapped bird fighting to get out.

"Another elderly woman," said Briar. "Imogene Parker, a retired politician. Same cause of death as Ellie Grenoble."

That was all I needed to hear. "Let's go." I grabbed him by the elbow, pulling him toward his cruiser.

"I'll tell the others you had to leave," Duke shouted after me. "Just keep me in the loop, Earth Angel."

I jumped in the cruiser as Briar got in behind the wheel. My mind was fixed on one thing now, and one thing only.

Another old lady had been stuffed full of dirt until she died.

Imogene Parker's house was a modest Cape Cod on the south side of town. Though she'd served as a county commissioner for decades, she'd never gotten rich—or married.

People had liked her, including me. Like Ellie, she'd visited Cruel World Travel, and she'd always been friendly and easy-going. For a woman in her eighties, she'd been healthy and energetic, getting around and living her life as if she were much younger.

Now, she lay motionless at our feet on the beige shag carpeting of her living room floor, a trail of pitch black dirt leading out of her mouth. Her denim shirt and black slacks were in disarray, half-unbuttoned and twisted around on her body. Her shoes and knee-length stockings had been pulled off and discarded on the sofa and recliner.

"She fought her attacker." Dr. Renee Cox, the medical examiner, took a sample of the dirt from Imogene's mouth and dropped it into a clear plastic vial. "Eighty-five years old, and she put up a decent fight. Good for her."

"Same killer, obviously." Briar scowled. "Same question of how they got all that dirt in the body."

"Was there a note this time?" I felt numb as I asked the question, dreading the answer.

Renee handed me a zippered baggie with a piece of paper inside. "Same as the last one," she said stiffly.

I help up the baggie and read the note by the light from the nearest window. My heart sank, because the text was identical to that left behind at Ellie's house.

Mother Earth is coming for the wicked. That was what it said, written in what looked to me like identical handwriting.

"Her home nurse found the body," explained Renee. "Showed up this morning for her usual visit, and there she was."

"No one else saw anything?" I asked.

"We haven't started canvassing yet." Marcus Greene, the patrolman who'd replaced the late Jim Withers as Briar's deputy, emerged from the doorway to the dining room. "But there *is* one of those webcams by the front door, which maybe caught something. We're waiting on the security company to send us video right now."

"Any cameras *inside* the house?" asked Briar, looking around.

"Not that I've found," said Marcus, scrubbing his left hand over his close-cropped black hair. "But I haven't been through every inch of the place yet, either."

Just then, as if on cue, I heard what sounded like a muffled cough somewhere below us. Everyone heard it, in fact, and looked at each other with sudden alarm.

"What about the basement?" asked Briar. "Have you been through there?"

Without answering, Marcus whipped around, rushing to the basement. Briar and I followed close behind.

Marcus flipped on the basement light and eased down the creaky wooden stairs with his service revolver in front of him, clutched in both hands. When he got to the spot where the upstairs walls ran out, opening up the view on both sides, he ducked down for a quick look with his gun at the ready.

He looked left, then bounced back up. Then, he looked right.

Then, he thundered down the steps with abandon, tucking his revolver into its holster on his hip.

As we raced down after him, we quickly saw what had gotten his attention. A huge pile of collapsed and broken cinderblocks occupied the far corner of the room.

A human hand stuck out of it, feebly twitching.

"We've gotta get this cleared!" Marcus started grabbing and heaving away fragments of block as soon as he reached the corner.

Briar and I followed his lead, though we knew there was a faster way to clear it. Our eyes met, and I knew we were on the same wavelength as to what to do next.

"We need shovels," shouted Briar. "Go get what we've got from the cruisers, Marcus."

Marcus cleared some more chunks of block from around the twitching hand, then turned and pounded his way back up the stairs.

Briar nodded at me and stepped back. I had already been gathering my energies and wrapping my mind around the debris, getting ready to make my move.

With a single soft grunt, I hauled off the front of the pile and cast it aside, letting the rubble crash to the cement floor. Now, we could see the person inside—another elderly woman, bruised and bloody and covered in gray dust. Her eyes were shut and her frail body pinned, contorted amid the debris.

Focusing my power, I lifted away the pieces surrounding her, heaving them across the basement. As I removed the last rubble holding her in place, Briar leaned in and caught her before she could fall.

I grabbed towels from a basket atop the nearby clothes dryer and quickly spread them on the floor. The woman coughed as Briar gently lowered her onto them.

"Call an ambulance!" shouted Briar as Marcus thundered halfway down the steps with two shovels. "Do it now!"

Marcus frowned when he saw we'd already freed the woman, then charged back up the steps with the shovels.

It was then that the old lady's eyes fluttered open, and she looked up at Briar. "Oh...thank God you're here."

She fell into another coughing jag, her eyes closed and her head and shoulders lurching up off the towel from the force of the hacking. Instinctively, I reached out to comfort her.

She opened her eyes, and her cough became a scream.

"Don't touch me!" she howled. *"Don't let her touch me!"*

"Calm down, ma'am," said Briar. "You're safe now."

"I'm not! *I'm not!*" The woman writhed on the towels, scooting backward away from me. "She's the *killer!* Oh God, she's going to kill *me,* too!"

The old woman's screams echoed in my mind as I returned alone to Cruel World Travel/Charmer Investigations. I couldn't stop thinking about the fear in her voice and the terror on her dirt-caked, shrieking face.

"Gaia?" Luna got up from her desk and approached me, looking concerned. "Are you all right?"

Duke, who'd been noodling around on his keyboard, followed suit. "Earth Angel? What's wrong?"

"There was a second victim at the crime scene," I said. "A survivor. She identified the killer."

"Whom did she identify?" asked Duke.

"Me. She said *I* killed Imogene Parker."

Luna shook her head in disbelief. "She must've been out of her mind. Too much trauma or something."

I nodded. "She was trapped under a pile of shattered cinderblock in the basement. It's very possible she has a head injury."

"Still." Duke took my arm and guided me to a chair. "Nobody likes to be accused of murder."

"Where's Briar?" asked Luna. "Still at the crime scene?"

"Yes," I told her. "The survivor wouldn't stop screaming unless I left, so...here I am." I'd driven around for a while after leaving the crime scene, trying to shake off the memory of her screams, but it hadn't worked.

Duke poured a cup of coffee and put it down in front of me. "I could think of several other possibilities for her misapprehension, my dear. For example..."

Before he could finish his sentence, the door flew open, and "Caravan" played. Briar stood there a moment, his face flushed, his jaws clenched.

"Gaia." His voice sounded cold and distant. "I'm sorry."

I'd just sipped the coffee and put it down slowly. A shiver coursed through me. "Sorry about what?"

Briar hesitated. "They sent the front door video, and there was video from inside the house, too. It shows the murder in...graphic detail."

Duke stepped between us, frowning. "And what does any of that have to do with the price of tea in China, good Sheriff?"

"Then there's the eyewitness." Briar leaned around Duke, keeping his gaze locked with mine. "And...other things, as well."

My heart raced as I listened. My feeling of dread intensified with each word from his lips.

"I'm sorry, Gaia." Briar walked past Duke, drawing a set of handcuffs from his belt as he came closer. "I'm sorry, but I have to take you in."

"*What?*" Luna was stunned. "This is *crazy!*"

"I know you couldn't have done this." Briar opened the cuffs and held them toward me. "I know there's an explanation for all of it. But I don't have a *choice* right now, given the evidence."

I looked up at him, fighting back the tears that were burning to escape my eyes. It was like a nightmare, the worst possible thing that could have happened between us.

So much for the well-deserved peace after our hard-fought clash with the Allself. So much for that vacation Duke had gotten me thinking about.

So much for the love of a sheriff for a woman with the weight of the world on her shoulders.

"All right." I rose from the chair and reached out, placing my wrists in the cuffs. He was kind enough not to make me turn around and wear them behind my back. "I trust you, Dale."

That was when he finally looked away.

"Gaia Charmer," he said. "You're under arrest for the murder of Imogene Parker."

The sound the handcuffs made as he slid them shut seemed like the slamming of a prison cell door to me. Still, I squared my shoulders and held my head high, refusing to look the slightest bit guilty as he read me my rights.

Though as he led me out the door to his cruiser, a tear trickled down my cheek, glittering as it fell like a single drop of rain to the earth beneath my feet.

ALSO IN THE SERIES